The Story of Lina Holt

A NOVEL BY
GINA V. KAIPER

THE DAYS & YEARS PRESS

PLEASANTON, CALIFORNIA

The Story of Lina Holt is published by

THE DAYS &YEARS PRESS
P.O. 10667
Pleasanton, CA 94588
Tel: 510-463-0468
Fax: 510-463-0481

Printed in the United States of America
10 9 8 7 6 5 4 3 2 1

PUBLISHER'S CATALOGING-IN-PUBLICATION DATA

Kaiper, Gina V.

   The story of Lina Holt/Gina V. Kaiper

ISBN 0-9645206-3-X

1. North Carolina—1865–1900—Fiction. 2. Populism—United
States—Fiction. I. Title.

Library of Congress Catalogue Number: 95-92564

Contents

Part Three: Death in the Midst of Life

Part One

Life in the Midst of Death

Chapter 1

April 1865

The name of William T. Sherman be forever damned. Ugliness is everywhere. The wounds run deep and will not easily heal, although nature is trying hard this afternoon. The grass in this meadow seems especially green and fresh, and honeybees slice through the air, on their way to the pear tree in bloom at the northeast corner. It was here that they found the sheep after the Yankees left last week—shot dead, all five of them, their wool stained with blood.

Lina Spruill shudders. Can't this sunshine soothe the pain and make things whole again? She sits for a moment on a stump and rolls up her sleeves to feel the sun's warmth. If this weather holds, the dogwood will open in time to decorate Bethany Church for Easter. There are plenty of folks this year who want a message of resurrection.

She gets to her feet again and takes up the split-oak basket. She is heading to the woods to cut some redbud branches for Mama, something pretty to set on the hearth, something bright to disguise the bareness of rooms stripped clean when the Yankees passed through.

She'll cut the redbud—and she'll think about Aaron Holt. She'll think about his brown eyes, and his hair that curls in spite of everything, and his soft mustache that arches down over his lips. Aaron laughing, Aaron talking, Aaron dressed in his uniform and ready to depart with his regiment that June afternoon four years ago, with his brother Charlie tugging him away, and herself left standing there, trying not to cry.

She has known Aaron Holt all her life. His folks live two miles beyond the crossroads, and his sister Flora is her closest friend, swapping quilt blocks and secrets (although her feeling for Aaron was a secret she never told, not until it was plain enough for anyone to see).

Surely she won't have to wait much longer to marry Aaron Holt. Surely some miracle will happen, and the war will end, and the Yankees will give up and depart, leaving folks to resume their regular lives again. She would like to be married in the spring, on a day like this. She would fill Bethany Church with flowering quince, and some of this redbud—she breaks off another branch and wedges it into the basket with care, lest she scatter the small pink flowers.

"Lina? Yoo-hoo, Lina—are you there?"

"Over here! In the woods!" she hollers in return.

It's her daddy, back from his rounds of the neighborhood. Ever since the Yankees came through, folks have shown particular care for each other, sharing provisions and news. This afternoon her daddy went to distribute some of his precious seed corn to families up the road.

Her daddy crashes through the underbrush. He is a thin, stooped man with reddish hair that's turning gray, and he still has a deep chest cough from the night he spent in the woods last week, hiding when the Yankees came through.

"They said at the house that they thought you'd come this way."

He seems uncomfortable.

"Well, mercy," she replies. "I guess they do wonder why I've been gone so long! I've been taking pleasure in this fine afternoon, and then I decided to fetch some redbud home for Mama. Pretty, isn't it?"

Her daddy takes no notice of the flowers but seems intent on speaking his piece, not wanting to be deflected.

"I've been down to the Holts'," he says. "Silas Holt just got back this afternoon. He took his wagon to Raleigh to bring Charles Wesley home from a hospital there. The boy got his leg shot off down to Averysboro, two or three weeks ago, or whenever it was, and Silas had just got word. I reckon the army was willing to let the boy go, seeing as how his folks lived so near—was glad to get him off their hands, I expect. Course, Silas had to go the long way around, lest the Yankees steal his mule."

"I had no idea that Aaron's regiment was fighting close to here!"

Charles Wesley is Aaron's older brother. The two joined up together and have fought together the entire way through.

Her daddy does not acknowledge her words and does not meet her eyes but keeps pressing on in a low and determined way.

"It was his left leg, and they took it off below the knee. It gives him considerable pain, but I reckon it will heal sufficient in time. Them two Holt boys have gone through this entire conflagration without a scratch, until now, until they came back near to home and their woes commenced. Well, sometimes the Lord performs His deeds in a slow, mysterious way—a way that doesn't always make sense to us plain folks with only mortal eyes to view the matter with."

He stops. That was a long speech for her daddy, and she does not interrupt, but she is suddenly frightened and grips the basket handle so tight that the wood cuts into her palm.

"Lina, my dear child…," her daddy says, his voice choking so that he has to stop and clear his throat. "Child, they think your Aaron is killed. In that battle to Bentonville. Charles Wesley wasn't there—he'd already been struck, three or four days before—but some other fellow he knew was brought to that same hospital where Charles Wesley was, and that fellow told Charles Wesley—said he'd seen Aaron lying dead on the battlefield, though he hadn't seen him fall. Course, it could be a mistake—lots of mistakes are made in war, and the Holts ain't seen a notice yet—but, child, I came right home to let you know. I am sorry, daughter—I am truly sorry. Your Aaron was a mighty fine lad."

The basket slips from her grasp, but she does not stoop to pick it up. The woods are in shadow now, and she's chilled. The birds are silent. Her daddy retrieves the basket and puts his arm around her shoulders. He leads her, stumbling, back to the meadow again and across the field.

"I expect you'll want to go over to the Holts' yourself," he says, "so you can talk to Charles Wesley direct. After supper, I'll hitch the wagon up. Mrs. Holt is entirely torn up, and I expect it might be a comfort to have you with them."

"I wonder," she cries, "why the Lord doesn't just strike me down as well, and be done with it, instead of dragging it out in pieces this way!"

"Lina, my child…," her daddy says, shaking his head. "What can I say? It ain't just, and it ain't fair—but then I ain't found much in life that is fair, when you get right down to it. It didn't seem fair to me when my first wife was taken away, leaving the boy and me."

She stops walking and looks at her daddy. He is both kind and tough, worn to the essence with beating himself against the odds—against the weather and the crops, against sickness and growing old—and now against this terrible war. He has known his full measure of sorrow.

6

"But why Aaron?" she can't help asking. "Why does it have to be Aaron?"

She sits on the wagon seat beside her daddy, a dish of honeycomb on her lap, the only luxury the Yankees spared, and it's little enough to bring. Sweet Aaron. Let him kiss me with the kisses of his mouth: for thy love is better than wine. It will be a long, long while before she can stand to read the Song of Solomon again.

It is not yet dark, but the ruts in the road are hard to see, and the wagon gives a sudden lurch.

"Are you all right?" Daddy asks, as he pulls the mule on course again.

"Yes," she answers. "Leastways, as well as I can be, under the circumstances."

A last delicate flush edges the clouds in the darkening sky overhead, and the evening star shines like a single candle flame. The chill of night is in the air, and she draws her shawl closer. Somewhere, ten or twelve miles in yonder direction, there are campfires burning in front of soldier tents. The Yankees are eating supper. And somewhere else, though she's not exactly sure where, Aaron's regiment is eating supper too. Without Aaron. She takes a deep breath to hold back the tears.

Her daddy pulls into the Holts' side yard, hitches the mule to a post, and helps her down. She takes the honey and follows him to the house and up the front steps. Silas Holt has come out to the porch.

"A sorrowful evening, Mr. Holt," she says.

He nods. Silas Holt is a heavy man, with dark eyes like Aaron. He too has been crying.

In the front room, where the family is gathered, Aaron's mother rises to greet her, and Simon P., Aaron's youngest brother, slides to one side to make room for her in the circle, next to Flora, who reaches out to clasp her hand. Never has she been so aware of Flora's resemblance to Aaron, but a softer female version.

"Where is Charles Wesley?" she whispers to Flora.

"In the other room," Flora says, "and asleep, I do hope. He's taking it pretty hard, what with the leg and Aaron too. But he'll want to see you, that's for sure."

She hovers in the shadows by the door while Flora sets the lamp on the table beside the bed. Whoever's lying there is restless and moaning. Suddenly he bolts upright, so fast that she gives a cry of surprise. Is that Charles Wesley? But he's so terribly thin! In the lamplight, the bones of his forehead and cheeks stand out with sculptured prominence, and his eyes look out from hollow caves. His hair is bushy and wild, and he has a full-length beard, not just a neat mustache. He is a pale, gaunt stranger—not Aaron's brother Charlie.

"It's me—it's Lina Spruill," she says when his eyes light upon her.

"Come here," he says.

She steps closer into the yellow glow of the lamp, trying not to look at the flat space on the bed where the hump of another foot should be.

Charles Wesley has talked to Aaron every day these past four years. He has slept in the same tent and has fought beside him all over Virginia and Tennessee. If anyone can keep Aaron alive, it is Charles Wesley. The boys were just a year apart. Aaron would be twenty-three come June, but she cannot remember when Charlie's birthday is. It doesn't matter.

"When did you see him last?" she asks. "What did you talk about? What did he look like?"

"It was that Thursday morning," he responds, "and we were drinking our hot water—didn't have no more coffee by then—and we were soaked clear through, standing out in the rain and getting ready to march. Aaron remarked about the temptation of being so close to you—just one county away, and he could walk it in one long night. And then the order was given, and we marched on down the road, and the fighting began. Next thing I knew, I was hit, and I never saw Aaron again. I keep praying that fellow was wrong, that it wasn't really Aaron he saw on that field."

Charlie puts his hand to his face, shielding his eyes from the light. Perhaps he is crying, she cannot tell.

"What was it like—the fighting?" she asks after a moment, hesitant to intrude, and yet she needs to know. He turns upon her a searing look, his blue eyes gone hard.

"It was pure and total hell!" he says. "Every single time. There wasn't any getting used to it—it was just something you had to do, and you hoped the Lord was on your side so you'd make it through one more time. You just formed the line and moved across the field, or wherever it was, with all the smoke and the noise, never knowing when it might be you. Course, I don't know what it was like for Aaron when he fell. Four years of fighting together, and then I wasn't even there. I feel so bad—Aaron dying, and me not even there."

He turns his head away.

"You couldn't help it," she says softly. "You were already hit yourself."

Charles Wesley flinches and draws up tight, as though pulling away from the scene.

"Yep, I was hit, all right," he says, pointing to where the foot should be but speaking so low she can hardly hear the words.

Silent and overwhelmed, she stands there twisting the cloth of her skirt back and forth between her fingers. The whole conflict has suddenly come home, here to this darkened room. Nothing will ever be the same again. With war, there is no going back. There is no way on earth to bring Aaron Holt back to life or to restore Charles Wesley's foot. All the high-flown talk, the flags and the uniforms—they are nothing. This is war. This emptiness. This aching ugly pain.

She turns to leave, but Charles Wesley begins to speak.

"Well, he sure might did love you," he says. "He talked about you all the time and carried your letters around—always kept one tucked inside his shirt for luck. Fact is, I expect there was one of your letters with him when he died, if that's any comfort to you, and I expect it's buried with him too. Your lovely innocent words—that's all he has with him now, wherever he is."

"And I loved him," she replies. "I loved Aaron Holt—and now what am I going to do?"

Chapter 2

July 1865

She is helping to plant a late crop of corn in the field that runs behind the log cabin where Will Coker and her sister Sallie live. This place fell into disrepair during the war, with Will away and Sallie and the child Lucy living back at home—nearly got burned, in fact, when the Yankees came through, but fortunately the fire went out, leaving only a long scorched streak at one end.

As soon as the conflict was over and Will was allowed to return, he set about working his land into shape once more. Some of the fields were already reverting to pine, but Will has borrowed her daddy's mule to furrow the soil. He is over there now, breaking up another stretch, while she and Sallie do the planting.

She follows the row, using a pointed stick to make a crater, then dropping the seed corn in. This is terribly late to be planting, and every hour counts in trying to bring a crop to completion, because if this corn is cut down by frost before it's come to fruition, how will Will and Sallie survive? Even so, it will take a heap of rabbit and squirrel to see them through, since Sallie's chickens aren't built up yet. No one has hens to spare.

Somehow, during all those months of wanting the war to end, she never considered that the aftermath could be so bleak—harder, in many ways, than the actual conflict itself. How simple-minded she was, to believe that once the shooting stopped, there would be food to eat and clothes to wear, that squabbles would cease and families could reunite in happiness to restore their lives again.

Instead, these past few weeks have seen yet more upheaval. Unruly bands—white and black—roam through the countryside, apparently unaware that there is nothing of value left to steal. It's worse in town, they say, with refugees camped everywhere, sick and starving. Perhaps the dead are not to be pitied. At least they are done with it all.

There are many days, even now, that she wishes she too were dead, that the smallpox or fever would claim her. At least then she would have some peace—and would be with Aaron again. Maybe she is coming down ill right now. There's a buzz in her head, but it may just be the heat. Or hunger, though even the thought of food makes her stomach wrench. She has had no appetite these past few weeks—especially for cowpeas, which is all they've had at home.

She reaches the end of the furrow and decides to replenish the sack of seed corn tied around her waist. She skirts the blackberry tangles that border the field and heads for the shade of a tree in Sallie's front yard. The child Lucy is playing there with a scrap of gingham and an old dry cob for a baby doll.

"Aunt Lina?" Lucy calls. "Her bonnet come off! Will you help me tie it on again?"

She is glad to humor the child and to rest herself. She folds the gingham in half and ties it around the cob. Then, on impulse, she searches the ground for pieces of stick to give the doll some eyes.

"Ouch!" She jabs herself by mistake, and she pinches up the flesh of her thumb to make a bead of blood appear. "Now I wonder, did I get a splinter?"

She is filling her sack with corn when a wagon appears on the road. Someone going to the grist mill, most likely, down by the river. There is no ferry, just the mill, where the road comes to an end.

She ought to get back to the cornfield but is glad for any diversion. She peers at the road again. Why, it's Charlie Holt! He stops and climbs down from the wagon, maneuvering with his walking crutch to break the jump. He leans upon the crutch, one shoulder higher than the other, and moves with awkward hops, his left trousers leg flapping above the ground.

Flora says the leg has taken its time to heal, but Charlie's face has begun to fill out again, and his beard is trimmed much neater now. She goes to meet him.

"Hello, Charlie," she says. "What you doing down this way?"

"Taking this corn to the mill," he says. "It seems that I'm the only one could be spared, since I'm not good for much of anything now, and everyone else had something of consequence to do."

"Well, at least it ought to be cooler, down to the river."

"You want to come?" he asks. "I need to talk to you anyhow—about Aaron's land."

The fifty-three acres on the other side of town that Aaron bought two years ago with his army pay. Fifty-three acres for Aaron, and fifty-three for Charlie, side by side. Charlie claims that Aaron's portion belongs now to her. He insists it's what Aaron specified, that they had talked about it a dozen times.

"It's just not right," she says, "for that land to belong to me, and I already told your daddy that. And, no, I can't go traipsing off to the mill, with all this planting to do."

The child Lucy, however, is dancing around and begging to ride, and Sallie too urges her to go. Half-reluctantly she unties the sack of corn from her waist and helps the child into the wagon bed, then swings up to the seat herself. Charlie offers his hand, the one that's free of the crutch, but she doesn't accept, and he scowls as he takes up the lines and signals to the mule again.

"I don't care what you say," Charlie resumes the discussion after the wagon is under way. "It's *your* land—that's what Aaron declared he wanted, if anything should happen, and I am bound and determined to see his wishes carried out. If you don't want to keep it yourself, then sell it. It's yours."

"Well, then, maybe I'll give it to Flora. Or maybe I'll give it to Simon P. It ought to stay in your family, it seems to me."

Why this incredible anger? She has no justified reason to be annoyed with Charlie Holt, yet every time she sees him, she is reminded anew of Aaron, and the grief wells up again. She sits rigid on the wagon seat, bracing herself with both hands against the bounce and roll. She does not want to pitch against Charlie.

"You ought at least to see it once, before you decide," Charlie persists. "That land was something Aaron deeply cared about—it was where he planned to take up farming and live—with *you.* I think you owe it to him to look it over. Surely you owe him that much, before you act so quick to give the whole parcel away."

She is crying again. She turns sideways, away from Charlie, and tries to blot the tears. These crying spells come upon her suddenly, with no warning, sometimes in the middle of the night, and she's not entirely sure why. Often she has not even been thinking of Aaron, but doing some task or another, when all of a sudden tears stream down her face. She doesn't want Charlie to see that she's upset, but the child Lucy is quick to spy the slightest aberration.

"Aunt Lina, why are you crying? Does your finger still hurt?"

"I'm *not* crying, so just you hush!" she answers the girl.

14

Charlie is looking the other way and doesn't appear to notice. Or maybe that's his kindness, to spare her embarrassment.

"It's just that I can't help thinking," she says, "how Aaron never got a chance to see that land for himself."

"Well, I told him about it often enough," Charlie replies, "and he certainly had it all clear in his mind—where he'd build your cabin and which fields he wanted to plant."

It was Charlie who took the furlough two years ago and came home to purchase both parcels of land. The boys had drawn lots between them, and Charlie won. Even now, the reminder of that twist of fate brings a jolt of agony. Why couldn't it have been Aaron?

"I suppose you're right," she admits. "I ought at least to go and see the place."

"Then what about this coming Sunday?" Charlie says. "If the weather's clear, my daddy and I plan to take the wagon, and I expect if you're along, then Flora will want to come. And you probably ought to ask your daddy, so he can advise you. He's a sensible man—he'll tell you it's a good piece of land, and that you ought to hold onto it."

"What time do you plan to leave?" she asks, half convinced and yet unwilling to let Charlie know.

"Right after breakfast," he says. "It's a right fair piece from home—maybe fourteen, fifteen miles. I haven't seen it myself again, since I been back home."

"Well, all right then—and I will ask my daddy."

Her daddy is sensible, that's for sure, and he has already expressed himself upon this matter, without even seeing the land. He says that she ought to honor Aaron's bequest, no matter how acute the pain, because Aaron will rest in heaven much easier for knowing that she has something to fall back on. If she winds up an old maid—and she'll never marry now, she's certain of that—then at least she'll have Aaron's land to bring her something in. She can rent it out, or sell the cordwood.

But no amount of land can take the place of Aaron himself. Dust to dust, and ashes to ashes—what good is a piece of land when life itself has ceased?

Sunday is hot but overcast. What will they do if it rains, and the wheels mire in the mud? This road is bad enough as it is—hardly a road, in fact. Just a widened horse path really, running through the woods. Maybe she shouldn't have come.

"I drove in a stob to mark the boundary off," Charlie says from the wagon front. "Course, there's no telling if that stob's still there."

Except for a pair of gutted chimneys, they have passed just one dwelling since they turned off the plank road, a log cabin where Negroes live. The woman stood in the yard and stared, her children gathered close.

"Well, here we are!" Charlie halts the wagon. "And, yep, right there's my stob!"

It's land, just ordinary land—that's all she can see. A narrow stretch of abandoned field, grown up in brush and with an occasional tree left standing, and then the woods beyond. But her daddy and Silas Holt and Flora are already down, and Flora, her sunbonnet flapping, is darting around and exclaiming over each stubby pine, each cluster of ragweed in bloom. She wonders at Flora's exuberance sometimes.

"Why, it doesn't look like it's even been farmed," she says, lifting her skirt to keep it from snaring on burrs.

"It hasn't been, hardly," Charlie replies. "The fellow that owned it had cleared just a few acres and planted a single crop of corn before he died. His main farm was a mile or so from here, and this parcel was how he planned to expand, except that he passed away instead. It was my Uncle Noah who heard it was up for sale."

"Then the land," her daddy says, "won't have had much chance to get worn out, so you ought to be able to raise yourself a right fair crop—I mean, that is, if you ever *was* to farm."

Her daddy is embarrassed, realizing his mistake. How can Charlie possibly farm? With one hand holding the crutch, and the other on the plow?

"And I *do* plan to farm," Charlie says, giving her daddy no time to repent. "Fact is, I'm moving out here to stay in another week or two. It's getting too late for a crop this year, but I'll set myself up a camp and get a good head start on clearing the brush away."

She walks away from the others. The land is perfectly flat, without a slope or a hill, and the clearing is enclosed by a dark strip of trees. It was the woods that Aaron loved the most, woods for hunting in, woods to find coolness on a summer's day. Aaron could imitate the calls of a dozen birds, and he delighted in finding a thicket where he could hide, and then whistle, eliciting a bird's response.

"If my recollection is true, there's some real fine hickories back through here."

She turns at the sound of Charlie's voice. He has followed her into the woods.

"I'll show you the spring," he says. "There's not but one on the place, so Aaron and me made it the dividing line between us. My piece runs back over there, and his begins right here."

A dark bubble of water trickles over a large flat rock and seeps into the leaves all around. Did nature place a stone right here, or did that previous farmer haul it into place? She stoops, and lets the water fill her cupped hands.

"Well, it tastes good," she says. "You're fortunate with that."

He nods, and squats for a drink himself, but awkwardly. The crutch is in the way, and he teeters a bit, on just the one leg.

"Charlie," she asks, "how in the world will you manage out here alone? Isn't it much too soon?"

"Oh, I'll manage, all right!" He stands back up again. "You sound just like Mama and Flora—trying to make me a cripple and a stay-at-home. Well, I already wasted four good years fighting that war, and I'll be dad-blamed if I'm going to sit around useless for the rest of my life!"

She stares at him, not knowing how to reply, silenced by his passion. Charlie starts off through the woods again, in the opposite direction from where they came, but he calls back over his shoulder.

"Well, come on, if you're coming! I'll show you where he intended to build his cabin—I'd told him about the spot."

He sights the sun, then crashes off to the right. She follows.

"Right here," he says when he stops. "Between those two big oaks. It's a natural place for a house, it seems to me, and Aaron liked the notion of building between those trees."

She looks at the oaks he is pointing to. They are tall, with smaller trees of all descriptions growing in between. There's even some dogwood here, and maybe redbud as well.

"This is the nicest spot on the place," Charlie continues. "We drew lots again to see who'd get it, but I made certain Aaron won. It seemed only fair, because I'd made the trip, you see. But, Lord, if I could only have seen what the future would bring, believe me, I'd have made absolute certain it was Aaron who came back home that time!"

"What's done is done," she says. "Maybe it was the Lord's will that I never see him again. Maybe the Lord is teaching me a lesson for loving Aaron too much."

Charlie gives her a peculiar, sideways glance, then turns to inspect the land between the guardian oaks. There are no stumps to sit on, but she drops to her knees on a clump of moss. She has asked herself the question a hundred times: Is Aaron's death her punishment, for craving him too much? For thinking about him all the time, instead of pondering ways to glorify the Lord? Is her love for Aaron like the Golden Calf that the Israelites set up?

"Well, I'll be blasted!" Charlie exclaims as he probes the ground with his crutch. "Somebody has built themselves a fire right here, and I expect I know who."

He spies something and bends to retrieve it, a small object, held between finger and thumb, a coin perhaps. Or a button.

"Yep, I was right." Charlie spits upon the ground. "Yankees! There were some of them gol-durned Yankees camping here, on me and Aaron's land! We were off yonder getting shot and killed, while them Yankees were sitting right here, defiling our land and roasting the chickens they'd stolen!"

He shakes his fist.

"Dad-blame it, but I *will* farm this place! So help me, I will!"

His voice rings through the woods.

"I *will* farm it, I tell you! And I intend to plow under every last remnant of them dirty stinking Yankees and their dirty stinking war! Just see if I don't!"

Chapter 3

February 1866

The next time she sees Charlie Holt is at Bethany Church on a cold Sunday morning when an icy wind sends gusts through the cracks of the small frame meeting house. She is not entirely surprised to see Charlie sitting there—Flora had mentioned that he might come home this week—but she has no chance to speak to him until the service is through.

"Well, Miss Lina, how do you do?" he says with a sweeping bow when she approaches the Holt family group.

"Hello, Charlie," she replies, wrapping her shawl tighter. "I know your family's right glad to have you home every once in a while."

"Yep, they do appear to be glad," Charlie says. "Mama and Flora outdo themselves in fixing me biscuits and ham. I tell them it's the victuals that keep me coming home, because there's only so much hoecake and roasted squirrel that a body can take, and I never was much of a cook!"

She joins the others in laughter.

"Well, nonetheless, Charlie, that hoecake must be agreeing with you, because you don't look near so peaked as you did a year ago—now does he, Flora?"

She turns to Flora for assent. It's amazing, in fact, how robust and healthy Charlie looks now. Even his beard seems to curl with extra vigor and life.

"Then it's work that's agreeing with me," Charlie says. "A little hard labor never hurt anyone, and I've done pretty good, I think. Got me five or six acres all ready to plow, whenever the weather agrees."

It is only now that she realizes what is so different about Charlie today: he is standing upon two feet, with his left trousers leg covering a boot, just regular, instead of hanging free.

"Charlie!" she exclaims without thinking. "You've got a leg again!"

"It's wooden," he mumbles.

"Charlie made that leg himself," Flora interjects. "And he did a real fine job—you can hardly tell. Charlie, show them how good you can walk with that thing."

There's a shift in Charlie's mood. He does not care to perform for the crowd that has gathered. Why torture him then? She starts to where her brother Benjamin waits, but Charlie calls her name and moves away from the others.

"Lina, it seems to me that *you're* the one looking peaked these days. I do sincerely hope you've not been sick."

"No," she answers. "Not sick exactly."

And yet not well either. No pains and no fever—only a sort of lethargy that began when Aaron died. How much weight she's lost she cannot tell. Food gives her no pleasure. Nothing really gives her pleasure any more.

"Anyhow, Lina, I'd like to ask your advice, if I may," Charlie says.

"About what?"

"About houses," he says. "I've got a bunch of logs cut, so I can build me a regular cabin instead of that makeshift shed I've used this winter. But now I can't seem to make up my mind. Should I use them as logs, just as they are, or

21

should I haul them to the sawmill in town and get them cut into boards?"

"Why, Charlie, do whichever you like. What kind of house do you want?"

"That's what I can't decide. A house built of boards is fancier—course, how fancy do I need, when it's only a room or two? And logs make nice thick walls and keep a place cool in the summertime."

"Then build it with logs."

"Aaron and I used to debate the matter—we'd go round and round, sitting there in camp. The house he planned to build for *you* was to be of lumber, and painted yellow. He had his heart set on yellow, for some reason I never understood. Sometimes in the evenings, he'd try to work it out. He'd draw himself a picture, deciding how wide the rooms would be and where the windows would go."

If only she had one of those drawings. Still, after all these months, she craves to know the smallest detail of everything that Aaron ever thought or planned. She yearns to know precisely what her life *would* have been like, if things had turned out different.

"Well, Charlie," she says abruptly, "*you* are the one who'll live in that house, so suit yourself."

All the way home in the wagon and most of the afternoon, as she sits by the fire and reads the Book of Ruth, she keeps coming back in her mind to a small yellow house at the edge of the woods. Somehow she has never thought that Aaron would want to paint the place—has certainly never pictured it yellow, but always muted to a weathered gray, like most of the houses around these parts. From now on she will make allowances for the paint.

There is a constant dream she has, always kept ready below the surface of her mind, a dream that she slips into whenever she has a chance. She and Aaron are in the cabin that he's built beneath the oaks, and she is cooking a stew with the rabbits that Aaron brought home this afternoon.

22

He sits cleaning his gun, and whenever she passes close, he looks up and smiles, or touches her hand. Sometimes the dream varies a bit. She is gardening or sewing or even scrubbing a floor, but always Aaron is there. Sometimes she tries to picture herself carrying his child, but she can never quite imagine how it would feel to have a growing creature inside herself. Bearing a child is another of life's experiences that will pass her by.

A hundred times these past few months she has wished that she and Aaron had been more impetuous—that they had married before he went off. Then maybe now there *would* be a child to share her loneliness, someone to care for and love, the way Sallie had Lucy during the war, while Will was gone.

The sharp pain of Aaron's death has receded, and catches her only now and then, but a huge flat emptiness remains. Sometimes she even suspects it's boredom she feels. There's always plenty of work to do, chores of one sort or another, but she has nothing left to look forward to. Nothing to plan for, nothing to hope for. She is twenty-one years old, and the best part of her life has already come and gone. If it weren't for her daydreams, in fact, she'd probably go start raving mad.

"Lina, are you all right? Were you talking to someone?"

Her mama startles her back to the present, to the Bible open on her lap. Mama is a short, dark-haired woman like herself, but heavy and broad, made wider-seeming by the thick gathers of her skirt.

"I'm fine," she answers.

She makes a great show of resuming her reading. She would be embarrassed for anyone, even Mama, to know that she indulges in daydreams like these—how frequent they've become, or how important. But has she started talking aloud to herself? Does she make strange faces? Does she gesture in the air, like some poor soul devoid of wits? Has she become an eccentric, someone that children shun?

"Lina, darling," Mama says, sitting down on the opposite side of the hearth, "you worry me a heap. It's not good to dwell on the past so much, when there's not a thing can be done to change a single lick."

"Yes, ma'am. I know."

But give up her memories, as few as they are? Give up this dreaming? That she's unable to do. The whole business has gotten out of hand, and yet the more she tries to restrain herself, the more these yearnings and dreams leap to the front of her mind. Somehow, she is reluctant to let them go—and not just for the loss of Aaron, strong as that feeling is, but also for the Lina Spruill she encounters there. The Lina she *used* to be, happy and content, the Lina who always noticed birds and flowers and butterflies.

Not this real-life Lina, bitter and obsessed, who's simply unable to rally her spirits any more.

Chapter 4

June 1866

She almost does not go to Charlie Holt's house-raising but changes her mind at the last minute because it will be a chance to visit with Flora. Except for church, she has scarcely been anywhere this spring, not even to town. The days have slowly eroded away, all the same except for slight variations in the chores at hand: churning, cooking, ironing. More than a year has passed since the Surrender, and the sharp edge of tragedy has been dulled by the rub of time.

It's been nearly a year since she last saw Charlie's land, but she notices the difference immediately. Corn and cotton grow thick in the fields, and the woods have been pushed back another few yards, leaving a trail of stumps to show where the trees used to be. Charlie has fenced in a hogpen and a vegetable garden. She had not realized his talent for neatness and order, but the vegetable garden is beautiful, without any grass or weeds. She has to admire it.

Her daddy and her brother Benjamin join the cluster of men beside the lumber that Charlie has piled to one side. The house will go in the open field, next to a sweetgum tree. Charlie has put up stakes and a string where the walls will be, and the brick foundation pillars already stand at each corner.

With Flora, she goes over to watch as Silas Holt and Charlie between them lift a long beam from the stack and hoist it to their shoulders. It's almost like a dance, the way they back up together and then move forward, maneuvering to where the house will be, except that Charlie walks with a limp, and his end of the beam dips with each step. Carefully they lower the beam into place, lining it up with the string.

"Isn't it amazing?" she says to Flora. "I mean how men can take a stack of boards and fit them all together to make a house that folks can live in?"

"I suppose so," Flora says. "But it's probably just as amazing to them, how we can take a length of cloth and turn it into britches or a dress."

Charlie's mother didn't come today, so only three women are here—herself, Flora, and Martha, Flora's younger sister. There are fifteen or twenty men, mostly neighbors from home, and all are busy now, carrying boards to Charlie's shouted directions. It's a wonder they don't knock each other down, with all that going back and forth.

"What you folks fixing for lunch?" she asks Flora.

"Mama fried up some chickens this morning," Flora replies, "and I made some blackberry cobbler—it's over in the wagon now. In fact, maybe we ought to move everything to the shade."

She helps Flora and Martha lug the box of food over to the trestle table that Charlie has set up.

"I'll take this milk and butter back to the spring to stay cool," she volunteers.

The woods are pleasant, the leaves making a roof of green. She finds the spring with no hesitation, since Charlie has cut a path and cleared the brush away. He has built a small stone springhouse too, and she sets the milk and butter inside, then dips her hands into the water and pats her cheeks, to feel the coolness.

Maybe she'll look at Aaron's land again. Quickly she comes to the spot with the two large oaks.

How many times this past year has she imagined herself right here? The place seems empty, in fact, without the yellow house. Often in her dream she is standing just about here and looking towards the house, and Aaron is chopping wood or harnessing the mule, so that she sees him across an open space that is dappled with sunlight. She tries now to conjure up a vision of Aaron coming through the woods, but the ritual seems fruitless and hollow. There is no Aaron here, and even his memory has blurred.

When she returns to the others, she is amazed to find that Charlie's house has each of the corners in. While the men are busy, she helps Flora and Martha gather scraps of lumber to build a fire in the yard. Charlie has a stove rigged up in his shed, but it's cooler to cook outside. She steps inside that shed to fetch a pot, and again Charlie's neatness surprises her. His cot is carefully made, his shirts hung on pegs in the wall. On the trunk beside the bed are a kerosene lamp, his Bible, and two or three folded newspapers. The shed is small, with a dirt floor and no windows. No wonder Charlie is anxious for a regular house.

By lunchtime, when the men gather to eat, the new house has bare studs standing parallel like ribs, with spaces where each of the windows and doors will be.

"Charlie, what you planning to do for heat?" her daddy asks, squatting, his plate balanced on one knee.

"That colored fellow whose cabin you passed is going to put me a fireplace in," Charlie says. "He hires out to build chimneys. Repairs them too—has done it for years, he says."

"Who'd he belong to?" one of the other men asks.

"Henley's been free for the past twenty years," Charlie answers. "But he had to buy his wife from old Mister William Cooper, who owns the sawmill at town. Said it took him four and a half years, and she was expecting before he got her clear—if the child had come any sooner, he'd have had to turn around and start paying all over again."

Charlie helps himself to another piece of chicken, then stiffly settles to the ground again.

"You folks out this way been having any trouble?" John Sanders, the first man asks. "I hear tell of niggers who call themselves soldiers and ride around with guns, flaunting themselves before the white folks. Course, the Yankees put them up to it—you can be sure of that."

"Them blasted Yankees!" Charlie exclaims. "You'd think they'd be glad the fighting was over and just go on back home! You'd think they wouldn't keep trying to run everybody else's lives!"

"I'm telling you, there ain't much room for an honest white man around these parts any more." John Sanders warms to his subject. "First thing, we ought to drive every one of them Yankees on back home. And then we ought to round up all the niggers and send them up yonder with the Yankees too. Or else we should ship them all back to Africa, and be done with it."

"Oh, it's too late for that," Charlie says, "because our coloreds are home-folks by now. It's the *Yankees* who don't belong here."

The older men have fallen asleep, stretched out on the ground in the shade, with their straw hats over their faces to keep the sunlight out. But Charlie and John Sanders seem eager to pursue their discussion. Charlie leans forward, his blue eyes sparking.

"Course, I have to admit that the Yankees are right in one regard," Charlie says. "Now that the coloreds are free, I think we ought to start teaching them what it means to be a citizen."

John Sanders frowns.

"First," Charlie proceeds, "we ought to teach them to read and write. Should have done that a long time ago."

"Why, we ain't even got schools for ourselves!" John Sanders exclaims. "There's plenty of decent white folks who can't even read a single word!"

"And second," Charlie continues, "we ought to give them the right to sign deeds—and to testify in trials and serve on juries, when the occasion arises."

"No, sir! Not on your life!" John Sanders quickly responds. "You'll never convince *me* that a lying, cheating nigger deserves the right to bear witness against a white man's word!"

The older men have all waked up. Everyone is alert and listening now.

"And third," Charlie says, "I believe we ought to give them the vote."

John Sanders leaps up, his face flushed.

"Now *that* is the final straw! That's just too blooming much! Charlie Holt, what in the name of tarnation was you up there fighting for?"

Charlie pulls himself to his feet. His face is as red as John's.

"Well, I didn't get myself near-bout killed so I could own me a slave, I can tell you that! I was fighting for justice and liberty—for the right of a state to be sovereign and free. Besides, I'm not so sure I'd do it all again."

"Charlie Holt, you are a *traitor* to the cause!"

Charlie flinches, as though physically struck.

"John Sanders, I am *not* a traitor, and you know it. You know good and well which side I'm on. But I *do* believe that the time has come to act with mercy and common sense, while we're setting things up again. And I believe we ought to take care of certain matters ourselves—without waiting for them dad-blamed Yankees to force us to it."

"Traitor! Traitor!" John Sanders shouts. "Well, I for sure don't intend to help some nigger-loving traitor build himself a house!"

Charlie does not reply, and no one else breaks in. The silence is intense. John Sanders and several of the others immediately go to their horses and wagons, but Charlie turns his back and refuses to watch as they depart in a cloud of dust.

Simon P., Charlie's younger brother, returns from the woods just then, where he'd gone to relieve himself.

"Ain't it time to get started again?" Simon P. asks.

"Yes, I reckon so," Charlie says, though obviously still disturbed. "I want to get the roof on at least—that's the part I'd have the most trouble doing alone."

"Well then, let's get to it," Silas Holt says, rising.

The men that remain get to their feet, stretching and bending, settling their hats into place and adjusting them against the sun. The hammering resumes, making a strange sort of rhythm, a series of cadences almost alike and yet not quite in harmony, like the separate songs of locusts.

She and Flora collect the empty plates, but the argument bothers her still. Surely John Sanders is not so foolish as to think that *only* Negroes are capable of lying and stealing. Surely the war just past has shown that yesterday's dearest brother can today perform the most treacherous deeds.

"Flora," she says as she lifts a basin of water to the table, "do you think they ought to give coloreds the vote?"

"Mercy, no!" Flora exclaims. "My brother is plumb-out crazy in some regards—always has been, and always will be, I reckon."

By the time the sun has dropped beneath the treetops and the men have ceased their hammering, Charlie's house is almost entirely blocked in. There are two rooms and a loft, although Charlie will have to floor the attic himself.

She wanders into the room that Charlie calls his kitchen and leans out the window that faces the sweetgum tree.

"Charlie," she hears one of the older men say from the other room, "now that you've got yourself a house, the *next* thing you need is a wife."

"A man doesn't need hot biscuits every morning to get along in life!" Charlie retorts. "Besides, I doubt there's a woman alive who'd marry a cripple like me."

As the wagons are being loaded, Charlie shakes hands with each of the men, and he kisses Flora and Martha on the cheek. This whole day, she suddenly realizes, Charlie Holt has not spoken two sentences to her direct. Until now.

"Well, Miss Lina," he says, as she climbs up to the wagon, "I hope you'll come back to see me, whenever you can spare the time. Or did that business today make you hate me too?"

"Land's sake, Charlie—you say the strangest things! Hate? Why, I've never hated a soul in my life!"

But riding home, coated with dust and tired from the heat, she probes her heart with a firm sort of honesty. Does she hate Charlie Holt? No, she finally decides. It is not precisely *hate* that she feels, although the turmoil he engenders is unexpectedly strong.

Chapter 5

September 1866

She is surprised to find John Sanders sitting on the front porch with Flora, and none of the other Holts in sight. As she climbs the steps, John Sanders gets to his feet, and Flora greets her with a hug. A pink ribbon is in Flora's hair, and a matching pink zinnia is pinned at the neck of her frock.

"Lina!" Flora exclaims. "What a happy treat!"

"I felt like taking a walk," she says, loosening her bonnet. "It seemed a shame to waste such a fine afternoon just sitting there to home."

"Pull up that chair yonder," Flora says, "and let's sit and talk for a spell. Mama and the rest are inside—though I told them there was no need to go running away, just because John Sanders happened to come stopping by."

John Sanders looks embarrassed, his narrow face deepening with color as he takes his seat again on the other side of Flora.

"Nice weather, ain't it?" he says.

"Mighty nice," she replies.

She cannot recall anything else of importance to say. No neighborhood news comes to mind—besides, she is not much inclined to gossip, not with John Sanders listening in. She is annoyed, in fact, to have walked all this way and found him here. Is he courting Flora? Well, obviously so, but this is the first she's heard of it. John Sanders' wife died of consumption while he was off to the war, and both of his sisters too. She ought to feel compassion, and yet she finds him a braggart and a bore. It's clear, however, that Flora does not share that opinion. Flora is laughing and fluttering even more than usual—she's provoked with Flora too, for acting such a fool.

A few minutes more, and she excuses herself. She passes straight through the house and out to the back porch, where the drinking water is kept.

"Oh!" she says, as she steps through the door.

Charlie sits there. He is whittling something, she can't tell what, and he is scowling. He does not seem to share her surprise.

"Good afternoon, Miss Lina," he says.

"I'm thirsty from my walk," she explains, and reaches for the dipper.

"That water's probably warm by now—here, let me get you some fresh."

Before she can protest, Charlie snatches the bucket away and limps down into the yard and over to the well.

"Thank you, Charlie," she says when he returns. "But I didn't intend to trouble you."

"No trouble."

He sits back down but folds his knife and lays the whittling aside. She takes a long drink from the gourd and then sits on the top step.

"Well, I'd best be heading back home," she says. "I promised Mama that I would cook supper tonight."

A simple lie. It is Bess's night to cook, but she cannot tolerate watching Flora any longer, and she certainly is not going to sit here alone with Charles Wesley. But when she gets to her feet and ties her sunbonnet on again, Charlie rises too.

"I'll hitch up the wagon and drive you home," he says.

"No, thank you. I truly prefer to walk."

"Then I'll walk with you," he says. "Unless you object, that is."

"You can suit yourself."

The road is partly in shade. Charlie's gait is awkward but steady, and she slows herself to his pace. They walk in silence the first half mile or so, but then Charlie begins to whistle, and finally he breaks into song.

"Come thou fount of every blessing…Tune my heart to sing thy grace!…Streams of mercy, never ceasing…Call for songs of loudest praise!"

It is her favorite hymn, and Charlie's voice is smooth and strong. At the end of the first verse he looks at her.

"Well, Lina, have you forgotten how to sing?"

That's a deliberate challenge. He knows full well that she used to sing with Flora in the church quartet but gave it up a while ago.

"Oh, all right!" she consents, and she takes up the melody, matching her voice against Charlie's.

The snap of fall is in the air, and colors seem unusually bright and intense—the blue sky overhead, the goldenrod in bloom beside the road.

"Well, what do you think?" Charlie asks when the hymn is through. "Do you think he's suited for her?"

"Who? John Sanders? Why, that's none of *my* business, I'm sure!"

"No, I reckon not. Anyhow, Flora's old enough to know her own mind. I wish her happiness."

Why did he have to bring the matter up? The singing had soothed her so that she was actually enjoying this walk, but now annoyance flares up again.

"You know, Lina, I would be much obliged if we could rest ourselves for a while," Charlie says, pointing toward a clump of trees in the meadow on the right-hand side of the road. His limp has grown increasingly pronounced.

To her astonishment, she feels completely at ease, sitting on a log beside Charlie Holt. But her thoughts keep returning to Flora.

"It must be awful bitter to you," she says, "to have your own sister courting a man you disagree with so violently."

Charlie's face darkens.

"Oh, we're not entirely enemies," he says. "I've already forgiven him for being pigheaded and wrong. And I trust he's done the same for me—though he hasn't specifically said."

"I just hope he treats her right." Her voice falters. "I declare, but I worry about Flora."

Charlie gets to his feet and turns to pull her up, but instead of letting go of her hand, he stands there, lightly holding her fingers. He looks at her, and she returns the gaze, until she feels a blush spreading upwards. Abruptly she breaks loose and runs across the meadow, her skirt catching on the weeds. She has to flee! She has to escape Charlie Holt! But when she reaches the road, she stops and looks behind her. Charlie is still in the meadow, a tall figure in patched blue trousers, and immediately she regrets her silly display. Charlie does not move as she makes her way back.

"I wonder did I leave something here," she says. "My handkerchief, perhaps."

She makes a gesture as though to search.

"Miss Lina," Charlie says, "one of these days you and me need to have ourselves a talk. I'd venture to say we ought to do it now, except that you have to get home and help your mama."

"Oh, I reckon supper can wait for a little while more."

She sits back down on the log. Half of her is skittish and nervous, wanting to fly away again—but the other half is amazingly languid and calm, as though she were perched in that tree overhead, beyond all danger and harm, merely enjoying the warmth of the sun. Charlie sits down beside her.

"Miss Lina," Charlie begins, "the next time I'm here to home, I'm wondering would it be all right to come and pay you a call?"

"Charlie, you know that my family is always delighted to see you."

"Now, Lina, I have great respect for your daddy, and I genuinely like your mama—but you know that's not what I mean. Would *you* like it or not?"

She glances sideways at Charlie, and then down at her lap again, almost giving way to the shakiness within.

"I expect I'd be right glad to have you come—in fact, I'm certain I would."

Her voice is so low that Charlie has to lean close to hear.

"Well, then," he states, "there's something else that I want to say. By next year, I'll have my place in right fair shape—and when that time comes, Lina, I hope you'll be willing to consider...well, to consider being my wife. Now I don't want to rush you, but I figure it's best to be plain about speaking my mind."

She does not reply. What can she say? She has certainly never imagined such a thing, and yet, now that Charlie has spoken, she finds herself not offended—but pleased. Shyly, she looks at Charlie and smiles.

This time, when he takes her hand, she does not pull away. When he leans over to kiss her cheek, she does not protest. Boldly, he kisses her mouth. O song of birds! O sweet September!

Then Charlie grows somber again. He does not speak Aaron's name, yet she knows who he means.

"I don't intend to destroy your memories of *him*," he says. "I don't intend to intrude upon your thoughts in that regard. But, Lina, you and me are alive. We've got our own gardens to tend."

He releases her hand.

"And there's one other matter that we'd best get straight right now," he says, sliding further away on the log. "I hope to heaven that it's not *pity* you're feeling. Because if it's pity you feel for me, then come right out and say it—and we'll stop right here. I couldn't abide it."

He ceases talking and abruptly rolls up his left trousers leg, revealing the wooden limb. It looks like the leg of an oversized doll, made of reddish wood that is marked with almost imperceptible ridges, left by Charlie's whittling knife. There is a strap contraption at the top to hold it on. Charlie unfastens the limb and removes it entirely, the boot still attached. He studies her closely.

"It's hideous, isn't it?"

His stump leg holds her riveted, and she reaches out to touch the rounded nubbin that ends below the knee. The skin is pink and taut, hardly like regular skin at all, and ridged by a jagged scar.

"Does it still hurt?" she asks.

"Sometimes. It goes up and down—following my moods, I reckon. But it doesn't hurt nearly as much as it did, and I try not to let it halt me."

He turns sideways, his back to her, and fastens the leg back on. Then he stands up and gives her a searing look.

"So there you have it," he says. "I want you to know the full ugliness of it, right from the start. Now, shall we call the whole business off, before we go down this road any further? Miss Lina, what do you think?"

She stands up and cautiously lays one hand on his shoulder.

"What I think, Charlie Holt, is that I'm already looking forward to the next time you're home again and coming to pay me a call."

Chapter 6

June 1867

Outside, a storm has broken, the rain lashing against the small frame church. The thunder creates such distraction that it's hard to concentrate upon the message that the preacher expounds. All around her people are restless, shifting about on the benches, getting up to lower the windows. The horses and mules hitched in the yard are restless too and make their own sort of commotion.

This rain is not an auspicious sign, and yet she finds a strange sort of pleasure in all this water pouring down. She looks to the opposite side of the church, where Charlie sits amidst his folks. He holds a posture of rigid attention, his head cocked to one side, as though this sermon is the only thing that matters right now, the only reason for gathering here at Bethany Church. Is Charlie nervous? She has not yet spoken to him today but purposely held herself back—not out of modesty entirely, but more from a sense of proportion. There's no need to be greedy for Charlie's attention because in just a short while more she will receive the gift of his entire devotion.

She herself is amazingly calm, and sits with her hands loosely folded. Around her, the Spruills and their kin take up three full pews. Even her great-aunt Dorcas is here, sitting beside her, a tall thin woman in a dark gray dress. Aunt Dorcas is delighted with Charlie Holt—but then Aunt Dorcas liked Aaron too.

The preacher ends his sermon, and the pump organ sounds the closing hymn. As she stands, she realizes that she cannot sing a note. There seems to be an enormous lump in her throat, and her stomach has turned into jelly.

"Daughter, it's time," her daddy whispers.

She nods, and follows him into the aisle, and Bess comes too. It is Bess who will be her bridesmaid—Flora was married at Christmas and is already expecting a child.

Now Charles Wesley is at her side. They do not touch, but she feels his presence in a physical way. Are his eyes still blue? Almost afraid to do so, she returns his gaze. Charlie, husband—the words seems strange.

The preacher opens his book and begins to recite. The litany is familiar, and yet it's as though she has never really heard it before.

> *For better for worse...*
> *For richer for poorer...*
> *In sickness and in health...*
> *To love, honor, and cherish*
> *Until death do us part....*

For the weather's mercy they must be grateful, although water still stands in the ditches beside the road. The rain ceased as soon as the wedding meal was spread, and a few brave people even carried their plates outside to eat beneath the dripping trees. She herself was much too excited to think of food, and now her stomach reminds her of its neglect.

"I declare but I'm hungry," she says to Charlie beside her.

"We can stop if you want to," he replies. "We can haul out that basket your mama fixed up. I'm right hungry myself—course, it's not but another mile or two."

"Then let's keep going."

Even that simple exchange brings relief. Somehow, once the chatter of departure ended, both she and Charlie lapsed into silence. The wedding seems to have made them strangers.

To Charlie, this trip is routine, a journey back to a house already familiar, a journey he has made a dozen times these past few months. But for her, it's setting forth across the sea. *Home* is still back yonder. This wagon even seems like a ship, creaking, rolling, loaded with everything a settler could possibly need: pie tins, pillows, and pickle crocks. There's even a crate of hens, covered with a quilt so the birds will think it's night. And the small gray-and-white kitten that Lucy gave them is crying itself hoarse, tied in a basket to keep it safe.

"What you going to name that kitten?" Charlie turns to ask.

He switches the reins to the other hand and puts his arm around her waist. She leans against him. Dare she lay her hand upon his knee?

"I haven't decided yet."

"Well, then, what you going to name our first child?"

"We'll name him Charlie after you."

Charlie grins and gives a hoot as he guides the mule off the plank road and into the sandy track that leads through the woods. They pass the cabin where the Negroes live and proceed a short while more, and then she sees it: Charlie's house—her house now—standing beside the sweetgum tree, its sides all blazing gold from the light of the departing sun.

"Just leave all those boxes and things," Charlie says as he helps her down. "We can haul them in later."

40

She is surprised, pleased, and a little embarrassed when Charlie lifts her in his arms and staggers through the door. For luck and prosperity, he says.

There's a double bed in one corner of the room, and a pair of straight-backed chairs beside the hearth, chairs that Charlie made himself. No curtains, no cushions, no hearth rug—not even a quilt on the bed, now that it's summertime. Only the fresh bare look of wood, swept scrupulously clean.

Immediately she moves to the kitchen. Most of the shelves are empty, except for a few chipped dishes, enough for a single man. But on the table stands Charlie's coffeepot, filled with a glorious bouquet, a bright abundance of phlox and marigolds.

"Why, Charlie, where on earth did you get these flowers?"

"I haven't the slightest idea," he says. "Unless it was Henley's woman, Josephine. You know—the colored folks down the road. She has a real knack for flowers, and it's Henley who's been seeing to my hogs."

What is it about a marriage that prompts such kindness, even from a stranger? Is it the business of starting out fresh? Maybe folks are glad for any new sign of hope, for any new journey that holds promise of a happy end.

"It's the prettiest bouquet I've ever seen," she says. "I declare but folks have been so kind. It's like a coverlet, isn't it? I mean all their blessings spread over us, keeping us safe and warm."

She leans over the table to smell the flowers. This is now her home. This is where she'll live with Charlie Holt for whatever measure of years the Lord sees fit to provide.

"Why, hey, Miss Lina!" Charlie exclaims, and he grabs her hand. "I haven't even showed you *my* gift!"

He leads her through the kitchen door and across the back yard, halting at the well. It is a proper well, built of stone and roofed to keep the sunlight out.

"Brand new!" Charlie announces, unlooping the rope to lower the bucket into the darkness below. "Me and Henley put this in for you last week. Now you won't have to tote water all the way from the spring."

Charlie hauls up the bucket. He offers her the first swallow—cold and good—and then lifts the bucket up over his head.

"Miss Lina," he proclaims, "here's to you and me! Here's to our future happiness! Here's to our crops and to all those children we're going to have!"

On impulse, she reaches out and grabs the bucket just as Charlie is tilting his head to drink, and the water sloshes over them both.

"Here's to flowers and to apple trees!" she says. "Here's to our new little kitten! And to chickens and to eggs—and to everything else I can think of! *Everything* that lives and grows!"

Chapter 7

August 1867

She sits on the back porch, shelling lima beans for dinner, wanting to start them cooking before she leaves for town. From here, she can see Charlie grubbing up a stump in the field across the road. Charlie is a hard-working man. Even at night, while she quilts, he is always studying some pamphlet about keeping bees or raising alfalfa. Or else he is whittling a piece of wood. By now she must have more cooking spoons than any woman in this county—in fact, there are two new spoons in her basket right now, ready to take into town.

She quilts, and Charlie whittles. She enjoys the evenings spent that way, with Charlie talking about what it was like in Virginia, about the mountains, the orchards in bloom, and everything else he saw while marching from camp to camp. And as he talks, his knife keeps shaving the wood.

But now Charlie has laid the grub-ax aside and is coming towards the house. He mops at the sweat that streams from his brow.

"Lina, are you about ready to go?"

"In a minute—soon as I'm done with these beans."

Charlie crosses the porch and puts his arms around her waist, so that she has to hold the pan of beans to one side.

"I'm missing you already," he says, "and you haven't even departed yet. If you want me to, I'll stop my digging and hitch up the wagon to carry you in."

"No sense both of us wasting a morning just for a spool of thread. Town's not so far but what I can stand to walk."

The morning is still cool enough to be pleasant as she walks along the narrow road that runs between the woods. In another week or so, the crops may be begging for rain, but for now they are doing fine. Henley Jones' corn—she is passing his place—seems about ready to pull. Henley's oldest child, a girl about the age of ten, is sweeping the front stoop of the cabin, while a baby plays in the yard.

The plank road is in such disrepair that it hardly deserves the name, but she follows the footpath that runs alongside. Halfway to town, she comes upon Josephine, Henley's wife, sitting in a patch of shade, with a small boy, about four years old, lying with his head in her lap. The child is barefoot and shirtless, but Josephine wears a pair of battered shoes that must have belonged to Henley, from the size of them. A yellow cloth is wrapped around Josephine's head, with a wide-brimmed cornhusk hat on top of that. Josephine is a tall, ample woman.

"Why, Josephine," she says, setting her basket down to rest her arm. "What you doing along here?"

"I'm toting this here truck into town," Josephine replies. "But I had to let my youngun rest himself. Missy, you headed that way?"

"I am."

"Then I expect we'll get moving along too."

Josephine nudges the child to his feet and shakes her skirts free of dust before picking up her bundles again. The three of them proceed single-file along the path—herself first, then Josephine, and last the child, who has to be constantly encouraged along.

44

"Josephine," she asks, "isn't this too much walking for that child?"

"Oh, he company," Josephine explains. "And besides, menfolks ain't so likely to mess with you when you got a child along."

"Well, it's safe enough now, with the war over."

"Missy—you white," Josephine gently replies.

She looks back over her shoulder at Josephine, who has one arm full of bundles and with the other is pulling the child along. How old is Josephine? Thirty perhaps? A slave until Henley Jones happened by. A good-hearted woman. She never sees Josephine but what she remembers those flowers.

"Josephine," she asks, "you got any family around these parts?"

"My brother, he still work for old Mister Cooper, but my poor mama took sick and died scarce a month after Jubilee. Never even had no chance to taste the notion of being free."

The sun has climbed halfway to noon by the time they reach the railroad tracks that mark the edge of town. They walk down a tree-shaded street, with houses along both sides, large houses that are painted white, with scrolled columns beside the doors.

"Old Mister Cooper's sister, she still live *there*," Josephine says as they pass the corner house, behind a fence of wrought-iron spears.

"You ever been inside?"

"Oh, yes'm—*plenty* of times! Old Mister Cooper, he just live around the corner."

"I expect it's right fancy, then."

"Fancy? Lord, but I reckon so! They has a teardrop chandy-lier that shines like a hundred stars! And a silver teapot, where Missy poured tea in the afternoons! But that were before the Yankees, and I couldn't say whether Old Mister Cooper's sister still has that teapot or not."

She parts from Josephine when they reach the main street and heads for Elihu Barnes's store. Elihu Barnes is busy, but when his customer leaves, she sets her basket on the counter.

"I've come to do some trading," she says.

Elihu Barnes is a man of mild appearance, with thin gray hair and a pale face. And yet, when it comes to trading, Elihu Barnes has at hand an entire collection of facial expressions. He peers into her basket, where a dozen brown eggs are nestled among unshelled lima beans.

"Them eggs fresh?"

"Yes, sir. Five was laid this morning, and all of them since Sunday."

"I ought to candle them and be sure," he says, frowning severely. "But I'll go ahead and give you a dime on the dozen."

He takes up a lima bean pod and splits it open, spilling the beans into his palm.

"I don't actually need any beans," he says, "but I tell you what—I'll allow you another ten cents for the lot."

"And the spoons?"

"A nickel apiece, same as usual, though I ain't sold the last ones yet. When you're dealing in spoons, the business comes and goes."

She is fingering a bolt of cloth, trying to decide between a solid red and a piece that's checked, to set off the barn-raising quilt she has planned, when Josephine comes into the store, lugging her tow sack. The child has been left outside. There are no other customers about, and yet Elihu Barnes appears not to notice Josephine's presence until she has pulled from the sack a square wooden box, and from the box has lifted a dozen eggs, each wrapped in a rag. Josephine carefully places the eggs on the counter.

"Where'd you steal them eggs?" Elihu Barnes demands.

"Naw, sir—I didn't steal no eggs!" Josephine protests, her voice unnaturally high. "My own hens is laid them, every one! I be Josephine! My man Henley trades regular with you but he ain't working to town today. The folks' chimney he building lives clear the other way."

"Henley Jones?"

"Yes, sir."

Josephine waits, her head lowered, while Elihu Barnes transfers the eggs to a wire basket behind the counter.

"All right," he says, "I'll allow you a nickel on them eggs."

"But last week Henley say you give him a dime!"

"A nickel," Elihu Barnes repeats. "You can take it or leave it—it don't matter a hoot to me."

"Yes, sir," Josephine whispers. "Then I reckon that be it—and I wants some coffee for my trading, if you please."

Elihu Barnes fills a paper sack with a single scoop of coffee beans, not even bothering to set the sack on his scale.

She watches through the open door as Josephine takes the hand of the waiting child and goes on down the street.

"Niggers—ain't they something else?" Elihu Barnes says, taking the bolt she holds and unrolling a length of red. "They'll rob you blind every time, if you give them half a chance. Now, Mrs. Holt, how much of this cloth did you say?"

"Three-quarters of a yard, and a spool of quilting thread."

She takes her parcel and goes outside, but before she has reached the end of the block, she turns around again.

"Hello again—you forget something?" Elihu Barnes asks when she steps back into the store.

"No," she replies. "I came back here to speak my mind. You talk about stealing—but I saw who was doing the stealing today. If *my* eggs are worth a dime for the dozen, then hers are worth that too. I can say for a fact that Henley and Josephine are honest, hardworking folk!"

She is trembling before the speech is through.

47

"Now, do declare!" Elihu Barnes says, not perturbed in the slightest. "Well, nigger eggs ain't worth but a nickel. But since you got yourself so riled up, I tell you what I'm a-going to do."

He takes another sack and spills in a handful of coffee beans, then twists the paper closed.

"Give that to your nigger friend, the next time you see her," he says. "And let me give you some advice, Mrs. Holt. There's folks who say that the war has altered your husband's mind and driven him loose from his senses—and you certainly want to be careful that the same thing don't happen to you."

Chapter 8

October 1867

Cotton-picking time. Charlie has come to the house al-most too tired to eat. In fact, he fell asleep on the porch while she was setting the table, and she had to shake him twice to rouse him for supper.

"How many pounds today?" she asks, as she spoons red-eye gravy over the crumbled cornbread on her plate.

"Right close to a hundred, I reckon," he replies. "But it's hard to judge from a tow sack—they all seem heavy when you're pulling them along."

"Well, that's the truth!"

She herself has spent every afternoon this week out in the cotton patch. Her back is killing her now. It hurts just to pick up a string from the floor.

Charlie protests her help. He claims that men and women have separate realms to tend. The house, the gar-den, the poultry yard—those are her domain. The fields are his. Charlie forgets that during the war many women had *both* realms to tend.

On Monday, after the noon meal, when Charlie headed back to the field, she went too—and told him she was only picking the cotton she would need to line her quilts. By

Tuesday, however, she managed to convince Charlie that they both would sleep better for knowing that the crop was safe in the shed. Reluctantly, Charlie agreed. Three acres of cotton is too much for any one man to pick alone—even if that man is Charlie Holt.

"I hope you're not planning to whittle tonight," she says, rising to clear the table.

"No," Charlie replies. "I haven't got enough strength to hold the knife."

When she goes into the front room, after the dishes are done, she finds him already asleep, with the covers pulled to his chin. His wooden leg stands on the floor by the bed, lined up with the other boot. Will they need a second quilt? It's turning cold in the evenings. She steps outside to the porch for a last quick look at the stars and stands for a moment, her arms wrapped in her apron, gazing out to the fields where the whiteness gleams like snow, even in the dark of night.

Fire, not snow. The house is on fire! Something is wrong! As she pulls awake, she realizes that Charlie, beside her, has emitted a strange and awful cry.

There is no sign of morning; the rooster has not begun to crow. Charlie repeats the sound, a cross between a wail and a scream. She tries to nudge him awake, but he does not respond. Shivering from the cold and her fear, she slides out of bed and crosses in her bare feet to feel for matches and lamp.

Charlie lies on his side, his arms tight across his chest. His face is contorted and pale, his lips drawn back as though clenched against some terrible pain. Is he ill? Is it the cholera? Has his heart given out from working so hard? Should she leave him here alone while she runs to ask Henley to fetch a doctor from town? O dear God in Heaven, please don't let my Charlie die!

"Charlie!" she cajoles, her hand on his brow.

She kisses a smooth patch of cheek above the roughness of his beard. Charlie twitches, and gives another cry, but more of a moan this time. His eyelids flutter. Gradually he grows aware of her presence.

"Is it your leg?" she asks. "Is it paining you bad again?"

"No more than usual, I reckon."

He shudders. She sits down beside him on the bed, clutching his hand.

"Charlie, if you're hurting somewhere, I want to know!"

"We were running," he answers at last. "We were running as hard as we could and yelling at the top of our lungs, like fiends at the edge of hell. And then I caught sight of Aaron—he was across a creek, standing under a tree as calm as you please, like there was nothing else going on."

He stares as though the vision is vivid yet. Then he resumes.

"His uniform was spick-and-span, like he hadn't even been fighting, and he didn't appear to notice *me*, or all the commotion either. I kept on running. I was trying to cross the creek and get to Aaron on the other side, and all around me, men were dropping like flies. And then the field burst out in flames, and my trousers leg caught fire...and my foot, my leg...."

He stops again. His eyes glitter, and sweat pours from his brow. She sits quietly beside him.

"That's the gist of it," he says finally. "There were other things that happened, terrible things—I just can't remember them all. Well, I guess it was only a dream."

Exhausted, he sits upright on the bed.

"Miss Lina, my sweet honey—I wonder would you do me a favor," he says. "I wonder would you fetch me a drink. I'm just too tired to strap that leg back on."

"Charlie, for *you* I'd walk to kingdom come and back—and gladly too."

Still barefoot, still shivering, she goes to the kitchen for a cup of water. When she returns, Charlie is crying, and the tears on his cheeks glisten in the lamplight. He takes the cup and drinks, as though swallowing the bitterest woe.

She blows out the lamp and climbs into bed. Charlie rolls over and clasps her in his arms. She strokes the back of his head, trying to console this man for the pain that racks him so. Is it Aaron he grieves for still? Or the loss of his leg? Or the war? Or all of those combined?

They lie together in silence, and yet they do not sleep. After a while she ventures to speak again.

"Charlie, how far is it down to Averysboro?"

"Thirty-five miles or so. Why?"

"Because I want to see it for myself—and maybe it would help you too."

He does not respond immediately. Perhaps she has made a mistake to bring the matter up. Perhaps the anguish would be too great and would only make things worse.

"Maybe so," he replies. "Maybe I ought to just go and confront the thing direct—soon as the rest of the cotton is in."

Chapter 9

November 1867

They have reached the other side of town and launched forth on a road that leads southwest. It is cold and crisp, and the stars overhead glitter with a brilliance unmatched by the lanterns that hang on the wagon front. The heated bricks beneath her feet and the quilt across her shoulders help keep the chill at bay but do little to ease her fear of the woods that press so close on either side. Even the mule seems alert, twitching its ears at the slightest sound. The road is rough, and progress is slow.

"Well, at least there's no mud," Charlie says. "And at least it's not likely to rain. Somehow, I keep expecting a flood, with blowing torrents of rain, like it was then. We were all of us soaked clear through. I don't know why the Lord saw fit to add such misery on top of our other woes. Course, the Yankees were soaked and muddy too."

The road leads over a creek, where a hundred frogs are croaking. Hidden frogs, with only their belching to mark their presence. She slides closer to Charlie on the wagon seat.

"I don't remember any frogs," he says. "And surely I'd have heard them, lying out on the ground all night, the way I did. Unless I was out of my mind—and I reckon I was, part of the time. But I expect it was just too early for frogs to be active yet. They were still buried in the swamp, waiting for spring to begin."

The sky has gone from black to gray, and with the growing light she can see both the woods and the individual trees, their heads still crowned with a last few leaves. The trees grow thick along this stretch. Occasional clusters of sumac, red with autumn, add brightness to the wayside, and in the open places, there's a hoary edging of frost on the ditchbank and over the fallen leaves. She glances at Charlie, but he seems oblivious to the wonders of nature and is focused instead upon something unseen ahead.

"Does any of this part look familiar?" she asks.

"We didn't march through here but approached from the other side. We'd been marching northward the day before, you see."

"You mean that Wednesday?" she prompts.

"Yep, Wednesday," he replies. "But it wasn't until the following day that my wound occurred—Thursday, March sixteenth—and I reckon that's a date I'll always carry in mind, though it was often hard to sort one day from another. Aaron and me kept track in a little book, so we'd know when the Sabbath occurred. In war, there's no special Day of the Lord—you're just as like to fight on Sunday as any other time."

"It was a Sunday," she says, "that Aaron was killed, and I hope the Lord doesn't hold it against him."

But she does not want to deflect his attention to Aaron. This is Charlie's journey. She has heard his story only in snatches, never from start to finish. He is reluctant, always, to speak of that final battle. And yet, if he doesn't speak, how can she comprehend? Even with telling, her knowledge can only touch the edge of what Charlie experienced. She can see only a blur, while Charlie perceives in sharp, minute detail.

The woods give way to open fields of empty cotton stalks, to farmhouses and barns where folks are beginning to stir. She shivers from the cold and takes heart at the rising sun, its light breaking across the tops of the trees. Charlie pulls the wagon aside, and they eat a meal of cold yams, washed down with coffee from a stoneware jug.

"I'd have been glad enough, then, for a yam—hot or cold," Charlie says. "We had hardtack and water that morning before the fighting began, and that was the last bite of food I tasted for near a day and a half. All night, while I lay out there in the rain and the dark, I kept dreaming and thinking about food. I wanted some coffee so bad I thought I'd die—and I reckon I near-bout did. It wasn't until after my leg was sawed off that I finally got some soup—one of the neighborhood ladies fed it to me."

They resume their travels again. In another hour they cross a river on a creaking bridge and pass through the village of Averysboro but keep heading south. Charlie seems puzzled and confused. He holds the mule to a slower pace and looks from side to side. Finally he stops altogether.

"There," he says, pointing to the right. "Over yonder. Do you see?"

What she sees is an unplowed field that's covered with broomsedge and weeds, and running cater-corner across the field are humped-up rows, like ridges left by the careless plowing of a giant.

"That's the breastworks we dug," Charlie says. "And it was hard enough to dig them too—what with the rain and the muck. We'd no sooner get ourselves a trench, then it would turn into a swamp."

Charlie pulls the wagon into a lane that crosses the far edge of the field, and he hitches the mule to a tree. He takes her hand, and they make their way back to the ridges. Charlie carries a long stick and swats at the weeds as they walk, occasionally turning up a piece of rotting canvas or a bit of tin.

"I carried my musket then," he says. "And we didn't have to worry about snakes—they weren't out sunning themselves that day."

The humps are nothing but dirt thrown up from a ditch, the ridges now grown over with milkweed and cockleburs. Charlie lies down flat in one of the ditches and pokes his stick over the top of the mound. She gets down beside him. From this vantage point, eyes just over the crest, she can see the road stretching ahead for another mile or so, until the woods close in.

"The Yankees came from that-away," Charlie explains. "And we were waiting for them here. Course, we couldn't see too far, on account of the rain. They were on horseback at first, and we were all on foot."

She tries to imagine a line of Yankees riding forward along that road, but all she sees is a tranquil autumn scene. It has turned out a beautiful day, and the sky is blue. In the distance, on the other side of the road, stands a two-story house. A Negro man is sawing wood in the yard.

"That was Thursday?" she asks.

"No, it was Wednesday afternoon that we first mixed with them here. Well, actually it was up there ahead a-ways, but me and Aaron weren't in the front line just then. The fighting yawed back and forth for several hours, but when it got too dark to shoot, the Yankees withdrew."

"Where did you sleep?"

"I'm not certain you can call it sleep," he says, "but it was somewheres back over yonder—over in those woods. There wasn't dry ground to be had, but me and Aaron propped our haversacks against a tree and wrapped our blankets around ourselves the best we could. We were bone tired from all the marching."

"Did you build a fire?"

"Oh, I reckon we built ourselves a fire—a small one. The Yankees already knew we were there."

"And then came Thursday," she prompts.

"On that Thursday," he continues, "the fighting began almost before it was light. They started yammering at us when you could still hardly see, and kept it up most of the day. First, it was up the road a piece, and then we fell back here. Push forward, fall back, and all the time it was raining cats and dogs, and the mud so thick we could scarcely walk without water running into our boots—those of us that still had boots, that is."

Abruptly he gets to his feet, picks up his stick, and moves across the road. She follows him into a grove of trees. Oaks, mostly, that once must have stood in grandeur but that now are broken and wounded, as though wracked by some furious storm. Branches grow at peculiar angles, and dead limbs hang overhead or lie on the ground below. She runs her hands over one of the gnarled trunks and discovers a half dozen lead balls embedded in the bark, as though a woodpecker had drilled them there.

Charlie, meanwhile, is wandering from one tree to another. Two or three times he kneels on the ground, his head flung back to the heavens, as though making an ardent prayer, but then he moves to another spot and does the same thing again.

"It was along here somewhere," he says at her approach, "but I can't seem to find exactly where. There were two large branches in a tree to my left that seemed to form a cross—I could see it from where I lay and took it for a sign, except that I was never certain whether it was a sign of hope or a sign of doom. I thought I'd never forget that tree, but I can't seem to find it now—everything looks so different today."

"Charlie, what time was it when you were hit?"

"Late afternoon. The fighting went on until dark, for another hour or so—first, right here around me, and then across the road again. Course, it seemed forever to me, lying there hurting, with my dead and wounded comrades scattered all around. The moaning and crying was something fierce—and I reckon I did my share of moaning too."

"Exactly how did it happen? What did it feel like?"

Charlie is pacing through the grove, looking upward every few steps, but he stops to reply.

"We were running forward," he says, "trying to drive them back again, and we were yelling at the top of our lungs, trying to make it seem like there was more of us than it was. I just kept running and tried not to mind the explosions all around—Lord God in Heaven, but I hope never to experience such a business again—knowing that death could strike with any one of those balls spinning past. But you just can't think about it, else you'd never be able to make yourself run at all."

"And then?"

Charlie has abandoned his search for the tree, and he stands with his eyes closed, both hands pressed against the sides of his head, as though trying to block the sounds of battle even now.

"Well, I was running forward, when something struck my leg and knocked me plumb to the ground. I thought at first I'd stumbled against a root, but it felt like my leg was on fire, and when I looked, there was blood, already running into the mud. I cried out, I reckon, but there wasn't anybody to lend me a hand, because the battle was still going all around."

He pauses, then resumes.

"I was mad as all get-out at first, to think some gol-durned Yankee should keep me from where I was wanting to go. But then almost immediately I felt a sense of relief. So this is it, I said to myself. This is what it's like to be shot, and I don't have to fear it any more. And then I started to pray—*Our Father which art in Heaven, hallowed be Thy name*—and then passed out, I guess."

She wants to take his hand but fears to break the spell.

"When I woke up," he says, "I thought for certain I was dead—it was dark by then, and quiet all around, except for the moaning and crying. But then I realized it was still raining, and I thought to myself that surely it wouldn't be raining, if this were heaven, and it wouldn't be likely, either, to rain in hell, on account of quenching the fires."

"So you lay there, and no one came?"

"That was the longest night I ever spent. I lay there crying and praying—drifting in and out of madness and dreams. They say your whole life passes before you when you die, and it's true. Mama, Daddy, Aaron, Flora, Martha, Simon P.—they were all there in my head, talking to me and telling me things I could never quite manage to hear. But then, when morning came, I roused up on my elbows and looked around, and there wasn't hide nor hair to be seen of my regiment. They'd all departed in the night, you see. Only the dead and wounded—ours and theirs—lay all around, and this grove was a sea of blood. It was the Yankees who finally came and lifted me out."

Charlie shakes his head, as though clearing away the sight. He seems to notice her again, and together they walk toward the two-story house. The Negro man has disappeared, leaving behind a stack of neatly sawed wood. There's washing hung on a line behind the house, the clothes bright in the sunlight, dancing with the breeze.

"This house was *our* hospital," Charlie says, stopping at the edge of the yard, "and theirs was down the road. When they carried me up those steps and inside, I couldn't help but notice a stack of arms and legs, piled like cordwood along the porch—I didn't know it then, but mine would be piled there too in a short while more."

The house appears to be just an ordinary farmhouse, with nothing special to mark it as a center of pain and woe. A washtub is propped upended on the porch, and a rosebush with one last scarlet bloom grows on a lattice beside the chimney.

"It was a Yankee doctor that did the butchering," Charlie says, "and I hated like hell to have them lay a hand on me—but by then I was just too weak to struggle any more. They said they were out of morphine, and they offered me whiskey, but I refused. So they stretched me out, right on the dining room table, and commenced to work. I could feel the rasp of the saw, but I was determined not to scream—not with Yankees there. I just prayed for the Lord to let me die, so the agony would end. *O Lord! O Lord! O Lord!* But of course I didn't die."

"Do you think there's folks at home?" she asks, nodding toward the house. "Do you think they'd mind if we came inside?"

"There's no need to disturb their lives any more," Charlie says. "I reckon they had surprise enough that day to last for a right good while. They were people named Smith—lots of Smiths in this neighborhood. It was an old woman named Smith who dressed my wound every morning and fed me something to eat—it was she who gave me the soup. A fat old woman, plain as sin, but she looked like a beautiful angel to me."

They turn from the house and cross the road again, back to the wagon. Charlie helps her up and then climbs up himself.

"They say old Billy himself came walking through that day, before the Yankees up and left. They say he came to inspect the damage his soldiers had done, but I don't recall him myself. Maybe I'd fallen asleep by then, or maybe it's just that the Lord took pity at last and spared me from having to look at the Devil direct."

As they roll through Averysboro again and over the creaking bridge, she sits close to Charlie, one hand in the crook of his arm. Oddly enough, Charlie begins to sing as they move along: "*Guide me, O Thou great Jehovah, Pilgrim through this barren land….*" She joins him in the song, and their voices float out together in the still autumn air.

"Well, that's all in the past," Charlie says when the song is through. "That's over and done, and there's nothing to do but to keep on moving ahead."

"Charlie, my dear husband," she answers, "I'll always be grateful to the Lord that He saw fit to have you spared."

He puts his arm around her.

"Well, Miss Lina, my sweet honey," he murmurs, "I myself often wonder, did He already have in mind for you to dwell close to my heart and make me happy in life again?"

Part Two

The Fullness of Life Itself

Chapter 10

July 1876

Waste not, want not. If she's heard Charlie say that once, she's heard him say it a thousand times. He even carved it into a board that's nailed above the kitchen door. Every bent nail must be straightened, and every scrap of paper saved. Even these pea vines will eventually be plowed under to nourish the ground again.

She tosses another handful of peas into the basket at her feet and turns to start down the other side of the row—but stops in surprise. A spider web is stretched between the pole and the string that holds the vines. Each delicate thread shines in the sun, although viewed from another angle, there appears to be no web at all. How can a simple spider weave such a lovely thing? How does that spider know when to retrace her steps and when to leap forth in an act of faith, hoping the thread will hold? She will skip the peas that hang on this vine. She does not want to destroy such handiwork.

"Children!" she calls. "Come and look at what I see!"

But the children are absorbed in their own affairs. Little Charles is out in the fields with his daddy, and the others are playing beneath the sweetgum, with four-year-old

Sophie in charge. Sometimes Sophie gets carried away with make-believe and forgets to watch the little ones. Then Robbie, the two-year-old, will seize his chance and streak clear out to the road. Jimmy-Jack, the baby, can crawl almost that far. She is astonished at the energy her youngest child displays. She used to lay him on a quilt but soon gave that up as useless and now is reconciled to having a baby who's dusty from head to foot, like chicken floured for the pan.

"Sophie!" she calls again, until the girl looks up. "Put that sunbonnet right back on, and keep your eye on the baby—why, just look a-there! Hurry now, before he swallows whatever that is!"

Children turn out so different—no two are ever alike. Little Charles has red hair and resembles her own daddy, while Sophie favors Charlie in an obvious way—the same light hair, the same blue eyes. Both of the younger two have inherited their coloring from her, with dark hair and wide dark eyes, and yet even the two of them are as different as night from day. Robbie is shy and quiet, and Jimmy-Jack just the opposite. Jimmy-Jack was puny at birth, but he is turning out to be the liveliest of all.

She has finished picking the peas and is down on hands and knees, pulling up beets, when Little Charles comes running in from the field. His face streams with sweat.

"Daddy wants you to bake us a cake for supper tonight!" the boy pants. "He says to ask you pretty-please!"

"A *cake?* What on earth for?"

"A birthday cake," the boy reports. "He says he doesn't care what kind you make, but he definitely wants a cake."

She rocks back on her heels. It's no one's birthday that she can recall, but with Charlie Holt you never know what to expect. Well, if Charlie wants a cake, then she'd better give extra attention to what she'll fix for the rest of the meal.

"And he told me to fetch him his book," Little Charles says, claiming her attention again. "He says for you to reach it down and send it back with me."

Charlie's latest passion is a U.S. history book, a heavy volume stamped in gold, that he purchased at an auction in the spring. It was a plantation sale, the family come to ruin, and Charlie had gone to look at plows but came away with the book instead. He is using it to teach Little Charles to read, although it seems a ponderous way to learn the ABCs, and the boy hasn't made much progress. Little Charles is going on eight, but there's no school close enough for him to attend, which Charlie declares is an absolute disgrace.

"Are you having a lesson this morning?" she asks the boy.

"He didn't say," Little Charles replies. "All I know is, Daddy told me to fetch him the book—he didn't say what he wanted it for."

Roast chicken, with cornbread dressing. Fresh peas, sprinkled with mint. Beautiful red beets, their greens cooked up as a separate dish. Biscuits, gravy, and preserves. And then the cake, iced in white, with a single red rosebud laid across the top.

All through supper it's been apparent that Charlie has something in mind. He winks at the children, and they giggle in return. But Jimmy-Jack, tied in his high chair, is beginning to squirm.

"Let me cut this cake," she says, rising to clear the serving dishes away, "so you folks can go ahead and eat, while I nurse the baby and put him to bed."

"No, not yet," Charlie says. "Lina, sit back down and leave the baby be—I want him to share in this occasion too."

Is Charlie going to read from the Bible, like he sometimes does? But it's the history book that he opens now, to a place marked with a leaf from a cotton plant. Charlie clears his throat and tilts the book to catch the fading light from the window and then looks up again.

"Do any of you know what day it is?" he asks.

"Yes, sir," Little Charles replies. "It's Tuesday."

"Yep, it's Tuesday all right." Charlie confirms. "And it's the fourth day of July, in the year of our Lord, eighteen hundred and seventy-six. And do any of you children know what *that* means?"

The children shake their heads. The baby throws his spoon on the floor and begins to cry. She lifts the child from the high chair and unbuttons the bodice of her dress. The child begins to suck.

"Well, this nation is one hundred years old today. A hundred years old—think of that! So we're having this birthday party in honor of the republic."

"Uncle John says republics do the work of the Devil," Little Charles interjects. "He says they do everything they can to keep the niggers all stirred up."

"Son, that's enough!" Charlie rebukes the boy. "I haven't got the slightest interest in what your uncle John Sanders says! He's wrong, and that's a fact. Anyhow, it's republic-*cans* he's talking about, and that's not the same thing at all. Now you children sit still and listen."

"When in the course of human events...," he begins, "...it becomes *necessary* for one people to *dissolve* the political bonds which have connected them one with another...."

Charlie gives a flourish to the words. He looks around the table, searching each child in turn, and he meets her eyes as well before his gaze falls to the book again. Charlie is so serious that she knows this passage, whatever it is, means a great deal to him. She gives it her closest attention.

"That *all* men are created equal…," he says. "That they are *endowed* by their *Creator* with certain *in*-alienable rights…."

Charlie stumbles over a few of the words, sounding them out. *U-sur-pa-tion,* for example. She has not the vaguest notion of what it means, but Charlie presses on, oblivious to the fact that Robbie is kicking his heels against the chair. She frowns at the child to make him sit still. Sophie, however, is listening to every word, her mouth hanging open. The girl dotes on her daddy.

"Well, that's enough," Charlie says. "At least we get the general idea."

He closes the book and puts it aside.

"What you reading from, Charlie?" she asks.

"That's what Mister Thomas Jefferson wrote to start the whole thing off."

"Why, Charlie Holt! I never thought I'd see the day that you'd be quoting a Yankee!"

"Mister Thomas Jefferson was no *Yankee!* Fact is, he lived just the other side of Richmond, and I've marched through those mountains myself. Besides, Lina, truth is truth, whether it's written by a Yankee or not."

The baby on her lap has fallen asleep, one hand still clasping the fold of her dress. Gently, so as not to wake him, she carries him into the back bedroom, the room that Charlie built on two years ago. Asleep is the only time that Jimmy-Jack is ever still. She kisses his soft clean cheeks before she lowers him into the crib.

When she returns to the kitchen, Charlie is relating some tale about Thomas Jefferson, to the children's delight. He has already cut the cake and passed it around. The slices are twice as thick as they ought to be, but then how often does someone reach the end of a hundred years. She tries to imagine what it must be like, looking back over such a span.

There used to be an old Negro woman, in the neighborhood back home, who lived to the age of ninety-eight. Why, she must have been a girl when Mister Jefferson wrote those words that Charlie read tonight! That old woman had shrunk almost to the size of a child before she finally died, but she was indeed ninety-eight. Her birth was verified on a bill of sale.

"Yep," Charlie is saying, "Mister Thomas Jefferson is one gentleman I intend to look up, if I ever get to heaven myself. There's a few questions I have in mind to ask him."

"But, Daddy," Little Charles interrupts, "you said the other day it was Stonewall Jackson you were hoping to see."

"Well, him too—there's a heap of fellows I'm planning to see. Course, I'm not entirely certain that they'll consent to talk with a plain dirt farmer like me—even in heaven. But then in heaven, there aren't any wars for men to be fighting in, and I expect there's no governments either, so who knows? Maybe Mister Jefferson will be right glad to stand around and talk, just to keep from getting flat-out bored."

Charlie laughs, and the children laugh too.

"Well, Miss Lina, my sweet honey," he says, reaching across the table to touch her hand. "Who are *you* planning to see when you get to heaven? And I know it's heaven you'll be going to, because you are certainly one beautiful angel, if there ever was one."

"Mercy, but I don't know," she muses. "I've never given the matter much thought. My daddy, of course…and Great-Aunt Dorcas…and Aaron. But I haven't got time to reflect on heaven now, with all these dishes to do. And, Charlie, these children have *got* to get to bed. Why, look at Robbie there! Poor thing, he's falling asleep, and he hasn't even finished his cake!"

Chapter 11

November 1876

The morning has dawned chilly and clear. The leaves on the sweetgum tree are a rich bright red, and it's a lovely sight. She turns away from the window to tie her apron on.

"What time are you planning to go and vote?" she asks Charlie, who has come into the kitchen after feeding the mules and the hogs.

"I'm not planning to go vote!" Charlie declares. "I've decided to let this election pass on by."

She is astonished. Pass up the chance to vote? Is this the same Charlie Holt who works himself into knots over politics and such? Who reads every newspaper and pamphlet that comes to hand? But before she can ask him why, Charlie stomps back outside.

What a disappointment. Election Day is a good time to visit and swap, and she has been looking forward to gathering with the neighborhood women, while the men do their duty.

She lays slices of ham in the skillet. Sophie is setting the table, but Jimmy-Jack, now beginning to walk, follows his sister and removes each fork and spoon that Sophie lays down.

"You stop that *right* now!" she says to the child. "And everyone get here to this table."

The children will be disappointed too. It's a shame to deprive them of the chance to play with other children. Sophie, especially, needs the pleasure of mixing with girls.

Should she ask Charlie to explain? Or would that only provoke him more? He has not spoken since sitting down to the table, and his demeanor is fierce as he spears a piece of ham and dips it into his grits. But Charlie brings up the matter himself.

"I'm still a-straddle the fence," he says, "and it's a most uncomfortable way to ride."

"What do you mean?" she asks.

"Well, I can't decide which way to go," he says, "and it's giving me fits. Neither side looks all that good to me. I doubt King Solomon himself could make a wise choice, this time around."

Democrats, Republicans, Conservatives, Unionists, Greenbackers, and Whigs. She has never known an election to be so disputed, with so many threats and connivings on every side. There was even a wild debate in town that Charlie attended.

"They say that Samuel Tilden is a decent, upright man," Charlie says. "And, fact is, I expect that's true. But voting Democrat in *this* state, at this particular point in time, is like voting to forget there ever *was* a war—it's voting to put things back exactly the way they were, with the exact same people in charge again, and the rest of us left to scramble as best we can. Somehow, I can't abide it."

Everyone agrees that the Democrats have one overwhelming intent: to put the whites on top again, once and for all.

"Well, you could always vote in the other direction," she says.

She suspects he's voted that way before, although Charlie has never admitted it, even to her. Most folks say there's not a respectable man to be found among the Republicans—that only a colored or a Yankee would ever hook up with that passel of thieves. Of course that isn't true, as Charlie has asserted a dozen times at least. Charlie says the Republicans have looked out for the common man—or at least they used to try. Voting and schools—those are two principles that Charlie believes in most passionately.

"It's not so simple any more," Charlie responds to her suggestion. "I'm not blind to what's been going on. I can't just close my eyes to all their wrong-doings and throw my ballot down the Republican road. It's an outright scandal they've made to Raleigh, and there's no denying it. Not to mention all those other corruptions up to Washington, D.C.—railroads, whiskey, and Lord knows what else. And I call it a *sin* to reward a man with gold, just for turning his head from one side to the other."

"Then why don't you vote for the *man*," she asks, "and leave the party be?"

"Because that's not enough," Charlie replies. "I'm not the Lord Almighty, who can see clear through the heart of a man. I'm just an ordinary mortal, so I have to judge a man, at least in part, by the company he chooses to keep. Why, you take Ulysses Grant! On the battlefield you couldn't have found a more direct and reasonable man— even most of *us* would allow him that—but put him in the White House, with all them turkey buzzards hanging around, and it's not been a sight to take pride in."

He pushes back his chair and hitches up his overalls.

"Well, this time around you won't catch *me* saying 'aye' to either side."

She sighs as Charlie goes back outside. She might as well resign herself to staying home today. But as she's drying the last of the dishes, Charlie comes into the kitchen again.

"I've changed my mind," he says. "I believe I *will* go vote, after all."

A dozen wagons and buggies are lined in front of Mount Moriah Church, and a fire has been built to one side of the yard, with benches set in a circle around the blaze. That's where the women are gathered. She takes her place among them and spreads her sewing on her lap, while the children dash off to join a game of tag. Even Jimmy-Jack, who doesn't understand the game, totters after the others, whooping at the top of his lungs.

Charlie joins the cluster of men on the opposite side of the yard, beneath the trees. With them are two gentlemen she's never seen before, men in fancy suits instead of overalls. One of the strangers puffs on a large cigar, and then she notices that most of the other men are smoking cigars too. The other stranger, a stout man, appears to be making a speech, and every few minutes he laughs aloud, a rousing chortle that carries across the churchyard and ends on a rising note, like a crow taking flight. Charlie, however, does not seem amused. Abruptly he breaks from the group and goes inside the church.

When Charlie reappears, he does not rejoin the men but comes instead to where the women sit.

"Lina, get the children and come on."

"Already? Why, Charlie, we haven't even...."

"I said *now!*"

Reluctantly she folds her sewing away. When the children are all collected, Charlie shouts at the mules, and the wagon pulls away with a jolt. It's clear that Charlie's dander is up. He sits erect on the wagon seat and pushes the mules to a rapid pace.

"Lina, I hope you observed that something mighty peculiar was going on," he says as they leave the church behind.

"Well, I did notice those two gentlemen from town. I don't recall seeing either of them before."

"Yep, they're meddling where they got no business, all right," Charlie says. "But there was something even *more* peculiar than that. Now think on it, Lina."

"I believe that was all I happened to see."

"Then I'll give you a hint. How many coloreds do you reckon there are, between here and Stony Creek?"

"Oh, fifteen or twenty families, I suppose—well, probably more than that, if you count all the little back roads."

"And how many of them did you notice there voting today?"

"Why, now that you mention it, I didn't see a one—and that *is* peculiar. Last time there were several that came along just while we were there."

"Yep," Charlie says. "Mighty peculiar. A dozen or so last time, and even more the time before. The way things are going, someone's liable to start running certain white folks away as well."

They lurch down the road towards home.

"Well, maybe I can't determine which is the best way to vote," Charlie says as they reach Henley Jones' place, "but I sure can tell the difference between right and wrong."

He gives a sudden pull on the lines and turns into Henley's yard. No one is visible outside except for a little boy the size of Sophie, who is dragging a stick in the dirt.

Charlie climbs down from the wagon.

"Son, is your daddy here?" he says to the boy, but the child appears frightened and runs away, out of sight behind the cabin.

Charlie knocks on the door. No one answers.

"Josephine!" Charlie calls. "It's Charlie Holt. I want to know is Henley here? Or is he working to town today?"

One of the window curtains moves ever so slightly, and the door opens. Josephine steps out and shuts the door behind her.

"I expect he around somewheres. Maybe out to the shed."

But before Charlie can turn around, Henley himself appears around the corner of the house, carrying an ax in one hand. The woodpile, however, is in plain view, and he did not come from there.

"Henley, you voted yet?" Charlie asks.

"Naw, sir." Henley shakes his head.

"Well, aren't you planning to?"

"Naw, sir. I ain't got no plans to go off voting today. I reckon I got more sense than to fool around like that."

Henley is being careful. The expression on his face does not change in the slightest, although he switches the ax to the other hand.

"Now, Henley," Charlie says, "there's no call to be telling me lies. Eight years ago you were shouting hallelujah because you folks had finally been given the vote, and when election day came along, *you* were the first one in line—I specifically remember. But today you tell me you've got no plans to vote? Well, I reckon I know what's going on— so go fetch your voting ticket, and I'll ride back with you. Course, they still might figure out a way to turn you down—I can't promise you they won't—but I *will* promise to see what I can do."

Henley does not budge.

"Naw, sir," he repeats. "I appreciates the offer—I is genuinely obliged—but I reckon I'll stay right here to home and mind my own business, so to speak."

"But, Henley," Charlie protests. "I'm telling you—if you folks let them take your ballots away now, Lord knows when you'll ever see them again! If I was you, I wouldn't let them get away with it, not without putting up a blamed good fight. So come on now—let's go."

Henley stands impassive throughout Charlie's speech, and when he talks again, it's with a patient tone, as though explaining something to his boy, who still lurks nearby.

"Mister Charles," Henley says, "like I done told you, I is genuinely obliged. But I got me a wife and eight hungry younguns to see about. Now, you could go with me to-day—and maybe them gentlemens would let me in, and maybe not. But if this here house was to burn to the ground one midnight, what then? Or if I was to suddenly get hurt so bad I couldn't even lift a brick, much less mortar it into place, and there won't no bread for these children to eat on account of it—what then? What then, Mister Charles? What then?"

"I don't know, Henley," Charlie replies. "But I do know one thing: if it's bad now, it's liable to get a heap sight worse before this whole business is through. There's just no telling *how* it will end."

Charlie returns to the wagon and hoists himself up to the seat. Henley, still holding the ax, watches as they pull into the road again.

The children, in the back of the wagon, are all agog. Little Charles seems ready to pounce with a question, but she holds him off with a look. Charlie is much too agitated to deal with the boy just now.

"At least," she says to Charlie as they turn into home, "you did everything you possibly could."

"No," Charlie answers. "I doubt if any of us has done what we really could."

Chapter 12

December 1876

"**N**ow, Mother Holt, you just sit still," she says, opening the oven. "I can baste this goose as good as you."

It is half past noon on Christmas Day, and most of the Holts are gathered at the homeplace—Charlie's widowed Uncle Isaac, Flora and John Sanders and their children, Simon P. and his bride.

Squinting against the heat, she lifts the heavy roasting pan to the top of the range and ladles drippings over the breast of the bird. Mother Holt, however, does not stay seated but comes to inspect the goose before it's returned to the oven.

"Another hour should do it fine," Mother Holt assesses. "So I reckon we can start on the biscuits. Lina, your biscuits are always so light, maybe you wouldn't mind mixing up the dough. I declare but I wish I knew how yours turn out that way."

"It's the buttermilk," she replies.

She can't help but smile to herself as she cuts in the lard. She well remembers the first time that Mother Holt came to dinner out to home, and how nervous she was—and how hard she worked to prepare an acceptable meal.

Mother Holt tasted each bite as though she were judging the entries at a fair. Few compliments were forthcoming then.

"Flora," Mother Holt is saying. "I'll ask *you* to mix the potato salad, if you please. The potatoes are already cooked and peeled—I let Eloise do that."

Poor Eloise, Simon P.'s new wife, has to live right here, under scrutiny every day. Mother Holt has definite standards.

She moves the rolling pin aside to make more room on the table, and Flora, as high-spirited as ever, begins to dice potatoes with a quick motion of the butcher knife. Flora's rosy cheeks give an impression of bustle and health, but when Flora opens her mouth to laugh, her teeth are rotted half away. No matter. It's always good to talk with Flora. They see each other so seldom—only on occasions like these, when the entire Holt clan has gathered.

"Lord knows, Lina," Flora says, "but all your children have shot up a streak since I saw them last."

"Yours too," she responds, arranging circles of dough on the baking sheet.

Flora's children—three girls, and a boy slightly older than Little Charles—all look like their father, with flat brown hair and pale narrow faces.

"I expect my Elijah is out yonder somewheres with Little Charles," Flora says. "I expect they're out there together, raising the devil."

"Well, I hope mine all wear themselves plumb out," she says, "so they'll sleep the entire way home."

In fact, she wouldn't mind curling up in the wagon bed herself, right now, to sleep for an hour or two. She has been so drowsy these past few days that she almost hoped it would snow last night so they could stay at home today, instead of leaving at daybreak and not getting back until well after dark. But now, she must admit, she is glad the day dawned clear. It's a happy pleasure to gather with folks at Christmastime.

But why is she so sleepy? Well, there *is* a reason, she suspects, and if it's what she thinks, it'll be apparent soon enough. She has not told Charlie yet, but he will be delighted—he always is.

"Lina, you look a mite pale, if you ask me," Flora says, mixing potato salad with a wooden spoon, one of Charlie's. "I expect you work too hard—you always did. Law, but you ought to take a lesson from *me!*"

"Yes, Lina, you *do* look peaked—you're white as a sheet," Mother Holt confirms. "Why don't you go rest for a spell? We'll holler when dinner is done."

"It's nothing," she insists. "I'm all right. Besides, it's Christmas, and I want to do my share. Now, Mother Holt, do you want me and Eloise to start in slicing those pies?"

The goose is done to golden perfection. The table is loaded with dishes, and some of the food is still in the kitchen for lack of room. It's a good thing Christmas dinner comes but once a year, else grown folks would burst out of their clothes as fast as children do. Her own dress already feels uncomfortably tight, although she hasn't yet eaten a mouthful—which of course is another sign.

"Son, will you offer the Lord our thanks?"

When Silas Holt says *son*, it's always Charlie he means, as though the family's hope rests solely upon Charlie. It was bad enough before Aaron died, but now it's gotten out of hand. Charlie, to his credit, never pays it much mind.

"O Lord, we thank Thee for Thy bounty," Charlie prays. "We thank Thee for this food and for the loving hands that prepared it."

The platters and bowls begin their journey around the table.

"Well, I hope that Seventy-Seven will prove to be a favorable year," Charlie says, helping himself to collard greens.

"It ought to be good," John Sanders replies. "To tell you the truth, I expect it will be the *best* year we've seen for a while—now that we've got things straight again up to Raleigh."

O Lord, please not politics, not here at the Christmas table. Despite all the years, the fray between Charlie and John Sanders has been only partially mended, and the slightest jar could tear them apart again. She looks across at Flora, who seems oblivious to any danger.

Thank goodness Charlie ignores the bait.

"Mama," he says instead, "your sweet pepper relish always reminds me of Christmas. It's the red and green together, I expect."

She sighs with relief and moves her knee against Charlie's, under protection of the tablecloth.

"Yes, Mother Holt," she leaps in, "I make a batch of relish every year, but it's never as good as yours."

John Sanders, however, won't let the matter rest.

"Speaking of Raleigh," he says, "it sure is a pleasure to have the Democrats taking charge again—and it looks like we'll have them up to Washington too."

"That's not been determined yet!" Charlie says.

How topsy-turvy this whole affair has been, and still not settled. First, it seemed that Mister Samuel Tilden would be the new President, but then the Republicans decided to count all the votes again. No one knows how it will end.

"Either way," John Sanders continues, "I expect the Yankees will finally pull out from here and leave us to ourselves again."

"And about time," Charlie concurs. "I just wish we'd hold ourselves to a forward course, without the Yankees to make us toe the line. But you folks have heard me

81

express myself on that subject before, so there's no need to repeat it all again."

Nervously she watches John Sanders. He takes satisfaction in keeping things riled up and is always eager to leap into argument.

"Yes," John Sanders says, "I believe we *have* heard you express yourself on the matter—time and time again, as I recall."

Charlie frowns but does not reply.

"Well, Washington or not," John Sanders continues, undaunted, "it sure might is a relief to have the *right* folks taking charge of things again. People know what's best— why, even most of the niggers have finally come around to seeing things our way."

"It was close, and don't you forget it!" Charlie retorts. "Fact is, I expect it was a heap sight closer than some folks would care to admit."

"Oh, it won't an absolute landslide, if that's what you mean," John Sanders says. "But *next* time, with the Yankees gone, and with the niggers keeping occupied in ways more suited to a nigger frame of mind—why, then I reckon we'll *see* whether it's close or not. I expect even the scalawags will come around in time—don't you think so, Charlie?"

She flinches. If there is any word in the human language certain to raise Charlie's ire, it's *scalawag*—as John Sanders is more than aware. She looks at Charlie. He is sitting tense and erect, his face flushed, but he holds himself in check.

"Daddy," Charlie says deliberately, turning to the far end of the table, "I wonder would you pass me another slab of goose. I declare but there's nothing so fine as the taste of goose."

"Dad-blamed scalawags!" John Sanders persists. "They're every bit as bad as the niggers. I don't see how any self-respecting white man in this state could look at things the way they do."

It is Silas Holt who brings the discussion to a halt.

"Now that's enough!" Silas exclaims. "I'd like to enjoy my dinner in peace, if you folks don't mind! I want to hear about something *else* on Christmas Day! Besides, the Lord Jesus Christ—whose birthday this is, as you may recall—never voted a single time."

Crops and the weather. Children and food. Old Mrs. Chester died, and her place is up for sale. The Binghams' barn caught fire week before last, and they only managed to save one of the mules and some of the hay.

By the time the pie is served, she is so stuffed that she can hardly eat another mouthful, but she takes a bite anyway and savors the taste. Is there anything on earth as good as pecan pie?

"Next year," Charlie says, "I plan to set me out a few more pecan trees, along the back side of my orchard. And I'm planning to raise a dozen hogs, instead of just three or four, and to plant a couple of acres in yams. Then if the price of cotton takes another dip, the way it did this year, I'll have something else I can sell. Besides, nothing can beat the taters we grow around here—even the Yankees admit to that."

Charlie likes growing as many different things as he can, and he is proud of his latest plans. He looks now to his father and to Simon P., but once again John Sanders feels called upon to reply.

"Cotton won't slide no more, now that the Democrats are getting things straight again. It'll *rise* this year, I'll wager!"

"Well, rise or fall," Charlie says, "that's more than any of us can know."

"Oh, it'll *rise*," John Sanders insists. "And rise considerably! Are you calling me a liar?"

"No, I'm not calling you a liar—I'm calling you a dad-blamed *fool!*"

She grabs Charlie's arm, but he brushes her aside. John Sanders, meanwhile, springs to his feet and lets his fork fall to the plate with a clatter.

"A fool, am I? Well, if you wasn't a cripple, I'd ask you to step outside, and then we'd just see who's a fool!"

Charlie stands up, already unbuttoning his sleeves.

"Charlie, sit down—I beg you!" she pleads.

"Lina, you keep out of this. All right, John—let's go."

She watches, aghast, as the two of them troop through the kitchen and out the back door. The rest of the family follows, even the children. She goes onto the porch and orders her four inside, but none of them obeys.

She cannot bear to see it. Charlie and John, face to face, begin to dance in a circle over the bare frozen dirt, with Simon P.'s hound dog barking wildly at their heels. Two grown men, who ought to be ashamed of themselves. Charlie lands the first punch, but John Sanders immediately responds in kind, and Charlie staggers backward. He recovers his balance and lunges forward, fists high, and they go at each other again, exchanging a series of blows before they move apart once more. Back and forth, around and around. There's blood on Charlie's chin, and his shirt is torn, his Sunday shirt. Fear and disgust rise in her throat, and Robbie and Jimmy-Jack, both clinging to her skirt, begin to cry.

"Stop them!" she hears herself scream. "Somebody do something—please!"

It seems forever before Silas and Simon P., between them, manage to break the two apart and wrestle them back inside, each to a separate part of the house—John Sanders to the sitting room, and Charlie to the kitchen. She wets a dishrag and wrings it out, but Charlie will not sit still. He spurns her efforts to wipe the blood from his lip.

84

"Lina, go get the children together," he demands. "I haven't got time to wait!"

"But, son," Mother Holt protests, "you can't just fly away, because we haven't even finished our dinner yet."

"Like heck, I can't!" Charlie replies. "I got no more stomach for pie—and there's not enough room in one house for me and that idiot both."

"Well, son, you'd have whipped him," Mother Holt says. "I just know you would."

Peace on earth. Good will to men. The sun has set, and the stars shine overhead, cold dancing points of light against the blackness of the sky. The children are all asleep, heaped over with straw and quilts, but she herself is shivering and miserable. She absorbs no heat from Charlie because she has slid to the farthermost end of the wagon seat. She and Charlie have not spoken to each other since they have been on the road.

It is Charlie who breaks the silence.

"All right," he says. "I'm sorry. I'm sorry that I let him get under my skin—and that I frightened the children and embarrassed you."

"He's kinfolks, Charlie," she replies. "Even if he *did* provoke you, and even if he *is* flat-out wrong. It's always easy to bust things apart—but awfully hard to mend them again."

"You want me to turn these mules around?" Charlie asks. "I'll go back and apologize, if you say so—provided the words don't stick in my craw."

"No, now that we've started, we'd best keep on."

But the mules seem terribly slow, the light from the lanterns sliding over their backs as they move. The wagon lurches from side to side, and it's making her sick. Abruptly she lays her hand on Charlie's knee and begs him to stop. He pulls the mules to a standstill, and she leans into the darkness and begins to retch. Pie, goose, and all. The entire Christmas meal.

Chapter 13

March 1877

Charlie is plowing her vegetable garden, and she'll go outside to join him as soon as the inside chores are done. This is the first day of spring, the day that they've promised Little Charles he can move upstairs to the loft to sleep. Then Jimmy-Jack can shift into Robbie's bed, leaving the crib vacant for this baby due in July. She has learned from experience that it's wise to do all arranging ahead of time.

"Little Charles," she says to the boy, who is fooling with a whirligig made from a button and piece of string, "we'll carry your things upstairs just as soon as I have these dishes done. But it would go a lot faster, son, if you'd fetch that towel and help me dry."

"I'm not a girl!" Little Charles protests.

"I'll do it, Mama! Let me!" Sophie volunteers, already dragging over a chair to stand upon.

"Well, whoever does it," she says, dipping a plate into the rinse pan, "had best be careful, because we got no money to spend on chinaware. So if any of these plates get broken, I'll have to feed you children from a pie tin down on the porch, like I do the cat."

The children laugh. For Jimmy-Jack, at least, the adjustment would not be great. He is madly in love with the cat, who tolerates the child's affection.

"Don't worry, son," she says to Little Charles, "soon as we're finished here, we'll get you settled in."

The attic stairs are steep, and in the loft itself she can stand upright only beneath the peak, although the boy won't have to stoop for a good while yet. The bed that Charlie made stands next to the chimney, and she plumps the mattress, filled with fresh clean shucks, before she spreads out the sheet.

"There's not much light at this end," she says, "but at least you ought to stay warm. Then when summer comes, we'll move you down to the window end."

She straightens up, pressing both hands against the small of her back. The child inside must have the hiccoughs again, a gentle tick in her abdomen. Little Charles is arranging his treasures—a rock that glints with mica, his jackknife, a whistle—on a board nailed between the rafters. The boy is growing up, there's no doubt about it.

"Up here," she says, "when it rains, it'll be like a lullaby. There's nothing on earth more soothing than the sound of rain on a roof."

Little Charles looks up.

"When there's lightning, will you let me come back downstairs?"

"Of course," she replies. "You know we're not banishing you, son."

She almost envies Little Charles the snugness of this loft. There's a fragrance to the place, from the herbs that hang from the rafters, and the floor is clean and bare, with no toys scattered about. Downstairs often seems cramped, especially when bad weather keeps all four children inside. This winter has been the dreariest she can recall, with a long cold rainy spell just after the turn of the year. Each of the children took sick, one after the other—and herself the sickest of all, although whether from influenza or from carrying this child, she was never quite sure.

But she doesn't want to think of that now. For every valley there is a hill. And winter, thank goodness, always gives way to spring.

Outside, there's enough nip in the air to warrant a shawl, but the trees in Charlie's orchard are on the verge of bloom, and the pear tree against the barn is already covered with white, the first to blossom every year. Some of the petals are blowing across the yard. Nature has an order for every living thing.

She is trying to discern if any pears have set when Charlie comes up, leading his mule to the barn.

"Well, she's all plowed and ready to go," he says, waving towards the vegetable garden. "I've done my part and am turning it over to you. And here—you'll be needing this."

He pulls from his pocket a folded piece of brown paper, the plan for this year's garden, showing where each vegetable should go, arranged by size and sun. Pencil marks indicate the rows—first planting, second, and third. Each spring Charlie works her out a different scheme.

"I doubt I'll get much done this morning," she says. "It'll probably take me another two days at least."

"You're getting some help," he says. "I've already told Little Charles he's to do whatever you ask him to."

Cabbage, squash, and okra. It takes a heap of plants to feed a family this size—and pray that the weather will cooperate so that everything turns out. Last spring her carrots failed entirely.

She slides the towsack she kneels upon further down the row. She is getting so large that it's hard to get down this way. With a quick, practiced twist of the trowel, she digs a pocket in the earth, drops a seedling into place, and pats the dirt smooth again. Little Charles is working in the row directly opposite. For a while he was singing to himself, snatches of regular songs mixed in with made-up tunes, but now he is silent, a puzzled look on his face. He has set his straw hat aside, and the sunlight gives his hair a deep red sheen.

"Mama," he says, "can I ask you something?"

"What, son?"

"How do you know there'll be another baby, come July?"

"Because I can feel it, son—sometimes, at any rate. And there's *something* growing inside me, that's for sure, and I expect it's a baby—I've never heard of a woman bearing something else."

"But how do you know it will get born in *July*?"

"Son, every creature has to grow for whatever time the Lord determines. It takes twenty-one days for a chicken to hatch, and four months for a pig, and nine months for a human child. So far as I know, that's how it's always been, and how it will always be."

She returns to her digging, hoping he'll let the matter lie, but Little Charles has never lacked for questions to ask. He keeps on now, his voice tightening a notch.

"What I *really* want to know," he says, "is how you decide when the nine months will start?"

She looks at the boy. His eyes are averted with embarrassment. Flesh of her flesh, and yet how much of this boy—of any child—is indeed of her own making? She and Little Charles kneel just three feet apart, and yet she can feel him growing up and away, into his own separate sphere. The boy is eight, although it seems just yesterday that *he* was the one moving in her abdomen.

"Son," she replies, "I expect you'd best ask your daddy about that."

"I already did, but he wouldn't say."

How can Charlie talk so freely most of the time, yet suddenly be at a loss for words? Surely the boy deserves an answer. She takes a deep breath.

"Well, son—you see this tomato plant?" she says, touching a seedling recently tamped into place.

"Yes, ma'am."

"Now, you take a tomato seed—as long as it sits on a shelf somewhere, it can't begin to grow. It has to be planted in the dirt before it can start making roots and leaves. Well, it's the exact same thing with a human child—it takes an act of planting, son."

She has the boy's complete attention.

"But on the other hand," she continues, "it's not *entirely* like a tomato. Because with human beings it's not just a case of getting yourself a packet of seeds, the way it is with these vegetables here. Now, I expect you've noticed that there's roosters and there's hens…there's hogs and there's sows. Well, there's men and there's women…."

She stops speaking. *He knows.* Little Charles already knows. It is written all over his face, mixed with a sense of relief. Then it's confirmation he's seeking—confirmation of what he suspects is true.

"Well, son, that's all I'm going to say right now, but I expect you can figure it out. Fact is, you already *have* figured it out, haven't you?"

"Yes, ma'am. I reckon so."

"But there's one more thing to keep in mind," she adds. "With humans it's not just something you mark on the calendar to do once a year, when the first day of spring comes along. Because with humans, the act of planting—well, it's one of life's pleasures, son. I hope you'll remember that."

"Yes, ma'am. I'll try to."

"All right," she says, picking up her trowel again. "Now let's get busy, on account of I want to get these vegetables in. Why don't we race each other, to see who's the first to finish their row?"

Chapter 14

June 1877

Scrubbing is torturesome, now that she's so heavy with this child, due in another month, but she intends to wash these sheets today, every one. All the beds have been stripped bare, and the mattresses and quilts are spread along the porch to air. Charlie and Little Charles helped her drag them outside before taking off to the fields.

This is the kind of day that's meant for cleaning house—sunny and bright—so these sheets should dry in no time at all. Tomorrow she'll wash the curtains and clean the windows, because if she waits much longer and the baby comes, then all summer long she will be doomed to looking at dusty curtains and panes.

She spreads a dripping sheet on the line, then glances over her shoulder at Sophie and the younger boys. All three children are peaceably at play, so she lumbers back to the washtub again. These days she reminds herself of a cow. Slow and lax, and really wanting nothing more than to lie in a meadow of sweet green grass. Cows don't worry about whether the sheets are washed, or whether the house is clean.

Each sheet gets twenty-five scrubs against the board. Ten, eleven, twelve…. Her back aches something fierce, and she pauses to take a deep breath. Thirteen, fourteen, fifteen…. She stops with a gasp at twenty-one. Has the washtub sprung a leak? Or has she merely sloshed herself? There's water running down her legs, and her shoes are wet. Her dress, petticoat, and drawers are drenched.

O Lord! O Lord!

She grabs the edge of the washtub as a sharp pain seizes her abdomen. It's the child! Her waters have broken! But she's not due for another whole month!

When the pain subsides, she abandons the unfinished sheet and heads to the house, clutching her stomach with both hands. Halfway up the back steps, she has to stop and catch her breath again.

"Sophie!" she calls to the girl, who is playing beneath one of the quilts spread on the porch. "Go find your daddy! Tell him to come right away, and not wait a minute—do you hear?"

"Where's he at?"

Merciful heavens! What did Charlie say he'd be doing today? Grassing the cotton? Or sowing cowpeas between the rows of corn? She sits down on the step as the next pain comes on. All three children watch, wide-eyed, as she bites her lip to keep from crying out.

"I think he said the cotton," she says when she's able to speak again. "So cut through the orchard—and hurry!"

Jimmy-Jack begins to cry as Sophie darts away, and Robbie is sucking his thumb again, but she pays it no mind. How much longer does she have? Each previous birth has gone faster than the one before, and if Charlie doesn't get here soon, Aunt Essie Taylor, the granny woman, may not make it in time.

"It doesn't help me one bit to have you children carrying on," she says to the frightened boys, who clutch her wet skirt. "Now both of you sit right here and be quiet until your daddy comes."

But they immediately follow her inside, and it's only with left-over cornbread, smeared with jam, that she's able to lure them back outside. Poor creatures. There's not likely to be a regular dinner cooked in this house today.

It's all she can do to hoist a pail of water up to table height before the next pain comes on, but she has to stoke up the fire and put some water on to heat. Nothing's ready. It's way too soon, and every sheet she owns is hanging wet on the line. She collapses onto a chair and begins to weep. Why today? And why isn't there anyone here to help? Tears spill down her cheeks before she manages to gain control of herself again. This is no time to be losing her head. She has to think what to do.

Bricks. She ought to heat some bricks and get a bed ready for the baby—except that the laundry basket is out there in the yard. She staggers to the door and leans her weight against the jamb, trying to keep her voice calm.

"Robbie, aren't you Mama's little man?" she says. "Well, I want to fetch my laundry basket and bring it here. I know you can do it if you try."

She has the basket in her hands by the time Charlie reaches the house, Little Charles and Sophie at his heels.

"The baby's coming!" she wails, when he bursts through the back door. "And there's nothing I can do! I don't even know if there's time to get Aunt Essie here—but, Charlie, please don't leave me alone!"

"Miss Lina, my sweet honey, I tell you what," Charlie says, even while he drags a mattress in the door and lifts it onto the bed. "Try to hold on just a little while more, and I'll be back before you know it. Fact is, I'll send Josephine or Henley to fetch Aunt Essie, and then I'll come straight back here myself."

This sheet that's tied to the bedposts is still half damp, but she grips it anyway and pulls with all her might.

"That a-girl, honey," Aunt Essie coaxes from the foot of the bed. "I can see the head now, so this next time ought to bring it clear."

Into the shadowy vale again. She pulls and pulls, as though only this one damp sheet could keep her from drowning in a torrent of pain. But at last comes another brief moment of calm, and she takes deep gulps of air. Surely the worst is over—she can feel it herself. And then, as though from a distance, she hears the first weak cry. But it's not until the afterbirth has passed that she garners strength to ask:

"Girl or boy?"

"I reckon it's a girl," Aunt Essie replies, her voice quiet and strange.

"Then we'll name her Lydia Mary, after my own mama," she says. "And can I hold her, please?"

"Ain't no one going to hold this child just yet," Aunt Essie replies. "When they're born ahead of time like this, you don't want to handle them any more than you can absolute help—nor bathe them neither, except to wash the birth slime away."

Thank goodness Aunt Essie is here. Aunt Essie always knows what to do.

"Welcome, sweet Lydia Mary," she murmurs, turning to one side and falling asleep.

It's late afternoon by the time she wakes. The light has shifted, and Charlie is in the room. He stands by the baby's basket, his back to her and his head bowed, as though in prayer. A quietness has fallen upon the house.

"Where are the children?" she rouses to ask. "I don't hear them."

Charlie does not turn around.

"I carried them down to Carrie Barnes—even Little Charles. She said I could come for them after supper or I could leave them to stay the night, either way, it doesn't matter."

"Did Aunt Essie leave?"

"No, not yet. She's there in the kitchen. She said she'd stay and help for a while, because every hour or so we have to change the bricks for ones that are warm."

Lydia Mary. The dear sweet newborn child, who she still hasn't seen.

"She's tiny then?"

"Yes, she's tiny."

Charlie sounds as though he's been crying. She cannot see his face, but he continues to stand by the basket, which is draped with a folded cloth.

"Is she beautiful?"

He does not answer.

"Charlie, I'm ready to see this daughter I've been waiting for! Bring that basket over here next to the bed."

Charlie turns around, and she's shocked by the stricken look on his face. She has never seen him quite this way.

"No," he replies. "It's best to leave her be."

It dawns upon her: *There is something wrong with the child!* She sits upright in bed and throws back the sheet.

"Charlie Holt, I'm going to see my daughter right this minute! So if you don't fetch her here, then I'll have to go over there!"

"All right," he answers. "I reckon you'll have to know sometime, so it might as well be now."

He lifts the basket with both hands and sets it on the floor next to the bed. Her heart thumps wildly as Charlie removes the cloth that covers the basket, and then the flannel blanket that's tucked over the sleeping child.

THE BABY HAS NO LEGS!

There are nubbins where the legs ought to be! The baby's eyes are shut, but now she moves one closely curled

95

fist. Charlie feels the pillow to see if it's warm and gently tucks in the blanket again, then drapes the cloth back over.

O Lord God in Heaven, why are you so cruel? She lies back and presses her hands over her eyes. Tears seep through her fingers. Charlie leans over the bed and strokes her hair, smoothing it away from her forehead while she cries. The sobs send ripples of pain across her abdomen. Gradually the room grows dark, and when the crying ceases, she lies there exhausted and spent. Charlie covers her hand with his.

"I'd comfort you, Lina, if I thought I could."

In reply, she brings his hand to her mouth and kisses his thumb. He tastes of salt, from her tears.

"What does Aunt Essie say?" she asks.

"Aunt Essie doesn't expect her to live, not more than a day or two. She can't tell for sure, but she thinks there's something wrong on the inside too."

Charlie loosens his grip on her fingers and turns his head away, his voice so quiet she can scarcely hear.

"Aunt Essie asked if I wanted her to start in feeding the child—or whether she ought just to let her be. Aunt Essie said that might be for the best, all things considering."

Silence in the room. Her own breathing ceases while she waits for Charlie to continue. Her heart is as fragile as the shell of an egg. It will shatter any moment now.

"I told Aunt Essie we'd treat this one the same as any child," Charlie continues, "and if the Lord sees fit to claim her again, then that's His business. Meanwhile, we'll do what we can. So we gave her some sugar water about an hour ago—and we're trying to keep her warm."

He lifts the basket to carry it back across the room, but she motions to him to leave it be.

"If this is the way it has to be," she says, "then I wish the Lord would see fit to tell us why."

"Because He's mocking *me*, that's why!" Charlie blurts out. "Can't you see that? Because He's not done with punishing *me* on account of that sinful war! Because the transgressions of the fathers have to be borne by the children—and this baby is the living proof of that!"

"No," she answers. "I refuse to believe it's on account of that."

She wakes from a fitful sleep. It is not yet dawn, but a faint suggestion of gray is showing through the window. The child was crying earlier, a faint weak cry that tore her heart in two, but now the room is quiet. Charlie has lit the lamp and set it on a chair next to the baby's basket—he hasn't done more than nap himself, ever since the child arrived, sharing with Aunt Essie all of the baby's care. Both of them lean over the basket.

"Is it time for another feeding?" she whispers, afraid of waking the infant.

Her milk has come in. Her breasts are painfully swollen, the nipples tender and sore, but she has not actually nursed the baby yet. Aunt Essie says the child is too weak to suck and has to be fed from a spoon, one drop of milk at a time.

"No," Aunt Essie answers. "She couldn't handle the last we give her—it didn't set right, somehow. And much as I hate to say it, I believe we're reaching the end. I doubt she'll last through the night."

"Are you certain?" she asks.

"Ain't nothing on earth ever certain," Aunt Essie replies. "But that's how it appears to me."

"Then if she's dying anyway, I want you to bring her here," she insists. "If nothing more can be done, then being held in her mother's arms can't do her any harm."

She sits upright in bed and smoothes the sheet over her lap. Charlie moves the lamp onto the bureau, where the light falls across the bed, and Aunt Essie wraps the child in a square of flannel. Aunt Essie hands her the bundle and tiptoes from the room.

With Charlie beside her, she holds the child in the crook of her arm and rocks her gently against her breast. All these months of waiting, and all the suffering and praying of the past two days, have at last come down to this. She touches the baby's cheek and runs her finger over the indentation where the bones of the head are joined. Covered by the blanket, the child seems almost normal. Ears, eyelashes, and fingernails, each in perfect miniature.

"It seems like a miracle," she says to Charlie, "that the Lord can work out His creation in stitches so small."

"I know it," Charlie says.

He too touches the child, caressing the brow, the hands. The minutes move toward morning, and the child lies still and pale within the curve of her arm. Yet when she touches the tiny fingers, they curl around one of her own. What instinct of nature gives a child the power to cling, right to the end?

"Silent night, holy night...," she croons, ever so softly as she rocks the child, careful not to break that fragile grip. *"All is calm, all is bright...."*

Sleep in heavenly peace.

Chapter 15

July 1877

"It's not right for me to sit here and watch you work," she says to her mama, who is cleaning the table after the noonday meal. "Idleness is not my custom."

"Now, Lina, there's no call to be pushing yourself so fast," her mama replies. "You'd best get your strength back whilst you can—besides, me and Sophie will have these dishes done in no time at all."

Mama gives Sophie a flick on the sleeve, and the girl starts gathering knives and forks into a pile. Sophie adores her grandmama—all of the children do. Mama has been here almost a month. Charlie fetched her the Sunday after the baby died, and a godsend it has been, to have Mama's comfort and help.

"Daughter, why don't you take your basket of quilt scraps out yonder to the porch," Mama says. "Me and Sophie will join you in a while."

Meekly she picks up the basket and goes outside, settling at the shady end of the porch, where the morning glory vines form a curtain of green. Today's blossoms have already puckered. Through the open window she can hear

Mama and Sophie, their voices weaving together, as Mama recounts some tale.

Using a pine lapboard, she places her paper pattern against a piece of calico and cuts out a row of squares. For days now, she has been cutting out patches. Somehow, it seems to lessen her grief, as though by smoothing these pieces of cloth, she is smoothing out her sorrow as well.

She lays out another block, moving the patches around, replacing one here and there. Sprigs next to solids, and darks next to lights. This past month, whenever she tries to think about the Lord Almighty, all she can picture is one huge quilt, like this one she's working on, only larger, with thousands and thousands of patches, of every color and description. And the Lord is studying His handiwork, taking up any odd scraps of cloth that come to hand and cutting them into shapes, trimming the edges, and then laying them here or there, arranging the pieces to make some pattern that only He has in mind. Nothing is wasted. Nothing is thrown away. Even the smallest piece of cloth, no bigger than someone's thumb, will eventually find a spot.

And her baby, poor Lydia Mary, is such a scrap, a tiny piece of pink-sprigged calico, already being laid into place somewhere. Oh, Lydia Mary! Her abdomen still mourns the child, and her arms too—sometimes when she closes her eyes, she still has a faint sensation of the child's weight in the crook of her arm.

Sometimes, though, she thinks that it was nature, and not the Lord, who took away her child. Nature is always making patterns too: night and day, summer and winter, life and death. Nature does not judge whether a thing is good or bad, and does not halt when mistakes slip through. An egg with double yolks, or a seed that fails to sprout. No matter. With nature, it's all the same in the end.

Charlie refuses to see it that way. He says there's no such thing as impartial, and no such thing as an accident—he believes everything that happens is the deliberate intention of the Lord Almighty. It has to be, Charlie insists, or else He's not Almighty, now is He? Charlie says every occurrence reflects the Lord's mercy or His judgment, one or the other, and sometimes both. But in her own heart she cannot accept the notion that Lydia Mary is a punishment for sin. What evil did she and Charlie commit, that the Lord would take such vengeance upon an innocent child? No, she cannot accept it.

"I told you we'd be done in no time at all!"

She looks up as her mama comes onto the porch, with Sophie right behind. Mama settles into a chair and fans her damp face with an apron. At fifty-seven, she is plumper than ever, her neck almost hidden by the folds of her chin.

"You want me to start in piecing this first one here?" Mama says, pointing to the quilt block arranged on the floor of the porch. "Provided those two little ones stay asleep for a little while more."

"Can I piece too?" Sophie begs.

The girl, her chair placed exactly halfway between herself and Mama, sits there fanning in perfect imitation.

"All right," she says to the child. "Go fetch your thimble, and I'll show you how—I expect you're old enough now."

"Five years old?" Mama says. "Why, certainly she's old enough. Lina, you were about that old when I started you in."

Sophie does not yet understand why the baby sister she'd prayed for so long should suddenly arrive—and then just as suddenly disappear. Ever since the baby's death, Sophie has been afraid of being nailed into a wooden box and carried away in the wagon, never to be seen again. No matter how often she reassures the child, a trace of suspicion remains.

She looks down at Sophie, her tawny hair spilling over her forehead as she tries to poke a piece of thread through the eye of a needle. Sophie sharpens the thread with spit and tries again. This time she succeeds, and triumph flickers like sunlight across her face. Sophie's moods shift as fast as Charlie's do.

All three of them—Mama, Sophie, and herself—are sewing when Charlie tramps through the house and onto the porch, carrying his straw hat upside down before him.

"I brought you-all a few cherries," Charlie says. "I hadn't even noticed they were ripe, but I've got Little Charles out in the orchard now, picking some for supper tonight."

He passes the hat to each in turn. A dozen ripe red cherries are in the crown. Charlie pops one into his mouth, then spits the seed over the edge of the porch.

"Daddy, did you see I'm quilting?" Sophie asks, holding up the beginnings of a square.

"That's my girl!" Charlie says.

He returns his hat to his head and disappears around the corner of the house. Ever since the baby died, Charlie has hovered close, stopping by every hour or so for one reason or another. Just checking, she suspects, to be sure that the Lord Almighty has not decided to strike another blow.

Chapter 16

September 1877

Some folks objected to having this meeting on the Sabbath, but Charlie and his committee insisted that they had to move immediately if they mean to have a school, or else the children will stay ignorant for another whole year. Besides, Charlie said, if it was set for a Saturday, there'd be folks who'd fuss about that. And having the meeting here at Mount Moriah raised still more objections, from the Hardshell Baptists and the Free Wills too.

She greets Carrie Barnes, now coming into the church with her husband Thomas, and Carrie slides onto the bench beside her. Carrie, a Hardshell, is the closest white neighbor to home.

"You folks have services today?" she asks Carrie.

"It's the Sabbath, ain't it?" Carrie replies.

The Hardshells don't have to share their preacher with three other churches, like the Methodists do. Brother Hosea Weaver is not a book-learned man but an ordinary farmer who one day heard the Lord calling him to preach—which he's done every Sunday since. In between, he continues to farm. Brother Weaver sits now on the opposite side of the church, arms folded across his considerable chest. He is scowling. He is probably passing judgment on this church with its small pump organ and its picture of the Lord's Last Supper hanging at the front. Hardshells hold no truck with such idolatries. Brother Weaver's right eye is glazed with a thick white film, and somehow, whenever she meets him, she can't help wondering exactly *how* that eye offended, that it had to be plucked from him so.

It's past time to begin, and Charlie is getting restless, but at last Will Johnson, in the front pew, stands up and clears his throat. Whenever there's a public meeting, Will takes charge—most folks expect it, and Will expects it too. His farm is the largest in this neighborhood. It was Will who gave the land that this church is built on, and who gave the pump organ too. A tall man, thin as a fence rail, Will Johnson is close to sixty and has no more children living at home, but both daughters live nearby, and his grandchildren would take advantage of a school.

"I reckon everybody knows why we're here," Will says, holding a sheet of paper in one hand, while with his other hand he tries to affix a pair of spectacles onto the bridge of his nose. "I reckon everyone's heard by now that the county has finally agreed to hire us a teacher out this way—on condition that *we* furnish a schoolhouse."

Will inclines his head to look over the top of his spectacles, and he clears his throat again.

"They've agreed to send a teacher out," he continues, "soon as the cotton crop is in—that's about six weeks away, but we have to make known right now what our intention is. Can we have a schoolhouse ready by then? Do I hear any talk on the matter?"

There's a shuffling of feet and some whispering from the back of the church. Charlie is leaning forward and rubbing his beard, and she is not entirely surprised when he's the first to leap to his feet.

"I'll give a wagonload of lumber," Charlie volunteers. "And you can put me down for six full days of work."

For years, Charlie has talked up the need for a school, and he has spoken of precious little else since word arrived from the county a week ago. Charlie sits down, and Brother Hosea Weaver pops up next, heading straight for the pulpit at the front.

"My good neighbors and friends," Brother Weaver begins, leaning upon the pulpit as though it were his own, "before we get ourselves all worked up about building this here schoolhouse that *some* folks are so all-fired anxious about, I want to ask you an honest question. I want to ask— do we even *want* a school? And, folks, I tell you right now, I have a heap of doubts. Thou shalt have no OTHER gods before me! What's to be taught in this so-called school? Sin? Corruption? Idolatry?"

"Dad-blame it!" Charlie mutters under his breath, but aloud he calls out: "Brother Weaver, I expect it'll be reading and writing—and probably some ciphering too!"

A few folks titter, but Brother Weaver, his voice louder, presses ahead. He has seized control of this meeting and left Will Johnson standing useless to one side.

"When Judgment comes," Brother Weaver says, slapping the pulpit for effect, "the Lord Gold Almighty, the King of Heaven and Earth, ain't a-going to ask who can read and who can write! No, sir! He's going to look straight into our hearts to see if we've accepted His blessed salvation! And, my friends, let me tell you, I'd a heap sight rather *my* children come to know the Lord's salvation than learn to read a single word! Now be honest with yourselves— hadn't you?"

Carrie Barnes nods in assent, and around the room, folks are already choosing sides, sensing a fight. And Charles Wesley Holt is not one to let folks down. He rises now, hooking his thumbs around his galluses.

"Brother Weaver," Charlie calls out, "*my* scriptures say we're supposed to love the Lord our God with all our heart...*and* with all our soul...*and* with all our MIND! Does yours say that, Brother Weaver? Does your Bible have that part about loving Him with all your *mind*?"

"Verily, I say unto you," Brother Weaver replies, staring at Charlie with his one good eye, "it is not that which *enters* a man that defiles him—but that which comes out of him! Evil thoughts! Covetousness! Wickedness! Deceit! And pride!"

"Brother Weaver," Charlie shoots back, "I'm sure you *do* agree that folks are supposed to follow the specific example of the Lord. Wouldn't you say that we folks here today should do the exact same things that He did, whenever we possible can?"

"Except ye take up your cross and follow me," Brother Weaver solemnly states, "ye SHALL not enter the Kingdom of Heaven."

"Well, then!" Charlie exclaims, and he too heads for the front of the room. He takes the Bible from the pulpit and flips through the pages.

"Yep, right here! Just like I thought!" Charlie exclaims, thrusting the Bible forward. "Luke four, verse sixteen...*and as His custom was, He went into the synagogue on the Sabbath day, and stood up for to READ...!* Well, Brother Weaver, what do you say to that? How do you reckon the Lord Himself could stand up there and *read*, unless He went to some kind of school? And surely, Brother Weaver, if the Lord Himself went to school, then we folks ought to make sure *our* children can do the same!"

Charlie closes the Bible. To her astonishment, the crowd breaks out in applause while Charlie returns to his seat. Brother Weaver does not even attempt to reply but sits down too, and Will Johnson steps back into the breach.

"I expect we're all in agreement now," Will Johnson says, holding up one hand until the room is quiet. "So let's move to the immediate business at hand. Now, six days of work has been offered, and do I have any more volunteers?"

Two days here, a sack of nails there. Piece by piece, it's the makings of a school. She is tallying the items in her mind when Carrie Barnes leans over and whispers: "You know, Lina, I wouldn't be the least bit surprised if someday the Lord don't call your *husband* to preach!"

She repeats Carrie's remark to Charlie that night, after they're both in bed, and he laughs.

"I have always wondered," Charlie says, "how a man can be so dad-blamed certain that it's the *Lord* a-calling, and not the Prince of Darkness in disguise."

"Well, Brother Weaver appears to have no doubts," she says. "Not about *that*, at least—only about everything else a body can think of to do."

She props up on one elbow. Was that a sound from the children's room? But whatever it was is not repeated, and she slides back under the covers and curls close to Charlie again.

"Tell me something, Charlie Holt," she says. "How are you planning to cut all that lumber and spend those six days working on the school—and still get our own crop in?"

"I'm not saying it won't be hard," Charlie admits. "It might even be so hard that I ought not to take any time to sleep. Fact is, maybe I'll get out of this bed right now and head on back to the fields."

He is teasing her.

"Well, Mister Holt," she says. "Tell me one more thing about that meeting this evening. How did you know what would be just the right thing to say?"

Charlie chuckles.

"Miss Lina, my sweet honey," he replies, "I'll tell you my secret. You see, I studied the matter out ahead of time, and I even worked me up a list of scriptures to use. Course, I didn't know specifically it would be Brother Hosea

Weaver I'd have to answer to, but I knew there'd be some-body. Always is."

"Charlie," she whispers, drowsy now, "since you're so all-fired smart, it's a wonder they don't ask *you* to take up teaching that school. In between preaching, that is. And farming. And anything else you take in mind to do."

Chapter 17

January 1878

The children have gone with Charlie to fetch Miss Beatrice Campbell, and now she can collect her wits and check through the house again. She does not want this meal to be an embarrassment. Miss Beatrice Campbell grew up in Fayetteville and not on a farm. But by now, she reminds herself, Miss Campbell should be getting used to country ways, although boarding at Will Johnson's is not the same as living on an ordinary farm, since Will Johnson's wife has colored help.

She circles the table, adjusting plates and spoons. She has laid out a clean checked cloth, with a bunch of holly from the woods to serve as a center bouquet. The front room is ready too, with a fire on the hearth and the bed covered with her brightest quilt. There is a certain pleasure in surveying a room where every single thing is dusted and clean. Still, no amount of sweeping—or imagining either—can turn this room into a parlor like Miss Campbell is probably used to.

She is nervous—awed by Miss Beatrice Campbell. She is not much accustomed to strangers, although by now Miss Campbell is really no longer a stranger. Her name has become a household word, mentioned no less than a dozen times a day by Sophie and Little Charles.

The meal is ready. The house is ready. She peers into the mirror that hangs above the chest, giving herself a last hard scrutiny. Dark hair, wavy and thick, that refuses to stay tucked into place. More and more she has come to resemble her own mother, although her face does not yet show all of Mama's character and grace. Nor, thank goodness, is she as plump as Mama. But isn't that Charlie's wagon she hears in the yard?

"Welcome to you, Miss Campbell," she says when Miss Campbell, Charlie, and the children burst through the door. "We're plain folks here, but I hope you'll make yourself at home."

Little Charles takes Miss Campbell's bonnet and coat and hangs them on a peg.

"My, something sure smells good!" Miss Campbell exclaims.

"It's the gingerbread," she replies. "The children requested that I bake it for you."

Baked ham. Collard greens. Stewed turnips. Candied sweet potatoes with raisins on top. Spiced peaches. Hot biscuits and blackberry preserves. It's a shame that she has to serve Miss Campbell such a simple meal, but in the dead of winter what else could she do? Miss Campbell, however, has been eating with great enthusiasm and is already helping herself to seconds. Doesn't Will Johnson feed the girl? If Miss Campbell consumes this much every day, how on earth does she stay so *thin*? Maybe it's because she's so tall. Or so young.

She is a bit astonished at this teacher the county sent. The schoolteacher she remembers from her own childhood was a pale and fidgety man, ancient before his time, but Miss Beatrice Campbell does not fidget and is not pale. And she has a bold head of hair, bright golden orange, plaited into a crown.

"Here, Miss Campbell," she says, returning from the stove. "Take one of these biscuits and butter it while it's hot."

She hands the plate to Little Charles, who carefully passes it on. Miss Campbell's presence has had an amazing effect on Little Charles, who seems to have suddenly matured by several years. Miss Campbell, she notices, calls him just plain Charles.

And Sophie too is acting unusually gracious. Sophie adores Miss Campbell and quotes her several times a day. Sophie won't turn six for another two weeks, and at first she herself was reluctant to send off a child that young to walk the three miles to school. But Sophie pestered Charlie to let her go, and it has to be something extreme before Charlie will ever deny the girl. Besides, Charlie said, there's no telling how long they can keep a regular teacher at hand, so Sophie ought to take advantage while she can. That was certainly the right decision, because Sophie caught on to reading as fast as Little Charles, and she writes far neater. But for Sophie the greatest enlightenment has been learning how to make paper dolls, something Miss Campbell revealed the second week of school. Sophie has been making the dolls ever since.

"Miss Campbell," Charlie now inquires, "Will Johnson says you're not but seventeen years old."

"Eighteen," Miss Campbell replies. "My birthday was the week before Christmas."

Why, hardly more than a child! It's a wonder her family has let her range so far from home. But then, she reminds herself, Mama was only sixteen when she married and already had her first baby by the time she reached the age of Miss Campbell here. But that's different. That's not living among strangers, and earning wages of your own.

"They say your daddy owns a brickworks down to Fayetteville," Charlie says.

"Yes," Miss Campbell replies. "He and his brothers do."

111

Miss Campbell winks at Jimmy-Jack, who sits directly across. The child has not taken his eyes from Miss Campbell this entire meal. Not once. Not even to eat. Neither he nor Robbie has spoken a single word since Miss Campbell stepped through the door.

"Well, bricks are mighty useful," Charlie says.

"My great-aunt Dorcas lived at Fayetteville a while," she turns to Miss Campbell and says. "But that was way before your time, and mine too. She had to come back up here when her sister—that was my grandmama—passed away. Still, she always spoke of Fayetteville as a lively place. I've never been there myself."

"Lina, your great-aunt Dorcas had a lot of gumption and spunk," Charlie adds. "Like Miss Campbell here."

"I don't know about gumption," Miss Campbell says. "Or spunk either. But I do like to see different places and try out different things. It's my goal, in fact, to see this entire country, from one ocean to the other, before I get old and die. I'm saving my teaching money for that."

"Is that a fact?" Charlie asks in astonishment, laying down his fork. "But surely you don't intend to go off traveling *alone*?"

"Why not?" Miss Campbell replies. "My plan is to teach here a year or two, and then try someplace else, further west."

"Oh, in a year or two," Charlie scoffs, pushing his plate away, "you'll be getting hitched to some lucky young man—a pretty girl like you."

"Well, he'll have to be a *traveling* man then, because I'm not interested in any other kind."

Little Charles takes this moment to blurt out: "Miss Campbell says that out in California there's trees that were already growing when Jesus Christ Himself was born! And there's mountains covered with snow, even in the summertime! And the *tallest* mountain in the country is there too, she says, but I forget how tall."

"Nearly fifteen thousand feet," the schoolmarm says. "Mount Whitney, in the Sierra Nevada range—and that's one of the sights I specifically intend to see."

After dinner, nothing will do but that Miss Campbell should climb to inspect the loft with Little Charles. And she has to be shown Sophie's quilt and Charlie's hand-carved spoons. What other secrets will the children trot out? And then Miss Campbell insists on putting her coat back on and trooping over the farm, not to be put off by warnings of briars and mud. Sophie and Little Charles personally introduce Miss Campbell to the cats, the dog, the cow, the mules, the pigs, and the chickens. In the orchard, Charlie shows her how he's grafted three kinds of apples onto a single tree. And the planting cycle of every crop has to be explained: cotton, corn, melons, yams, sorghum, cowpeas, and peanuts.

The sun is angled low before Charlie hitches the wagon to carry Miss Campbell back to Will Johnson's again. The children clamor to go along, and Charlie agrees—except for Jimmy-Jack, who is showing strain from the lack of a nap. She and Jimmy-Jack watch from the window as the wagon pulls away, Miss Campbell on the seat next to Charlie, her hair ablaze with the final rays of the sun. Miss Campbell and the children wave, and she and Jimmy-Jack wave in return.

The house seems amazingly empty and quiet. She lays another piece of wood on the fire and settles into the rocking chair. She ought to go feed her hens, but she is worn out from being on display and from all those questions and facts, hurled hither and yon. The wood catches, and sends dancing streaks of light up the walls. Jimmy-Jack climbs onto her lap and rests his head against her breast, and she wraps her arms around him.

"Jimmy-Jack go to school," the child murmurs, almost asleep.

"Oh, not for a while, my pet," she says, stroking his curly hair, dark like her own. "And by then Miss Beatrice Campbell will be long gone from here. She'll be off to Lord knows where, climbing mountains and such. *That's* where Miss Beatrice Campbell will be."

Chapter 18

May 1878

Pregnant again, she's almost sure. She lies awake in the early gray dawn, trying to decide what makes her so certain. And yet she *is* certain. By now, she has learned to decipher each subtle shift that her body makes: a little swelling here, a spot of tenderness there.

The only question is when. Christmastime perhaps. She counts off the months on her fingers—no, later than that. January.

And a girl or a boy? Another boy, most likely, if what folks say is true, that in the aftermath of war, nature replenishes the stock. Well, she's done her share towards restoring the balance again. Did the Hebrew women of Moses' time bear more males, after the Pharaoh's slaughter? Charlie might know.

She rolls on her side and looks at Charlie, still asleep, his face now visible in the growing light, his beard and tousled hair forming a frame around the smoother planes of his skin. His forehead, higher than it used to be, is slightly furrowed, as though marked with a small invisible plow. It amuses her to think of Charlie's face as a plot of land, with the wilderness threatening to encroach upon the fields again. They are growing older, both of them.

And on the other side of Charlie, she can see his uniform, hung on the back of a chair, brushed and ready—the gray wool coat and the tilt-topped hat. His boots were rubbed with neat's foot oil last night, and they wait too, the one that holds his leg standing upright next to the chair. Each year, on this same day, the veterans from all around march through the center of town, and Charlie Holt is always among them. For reasons that she does not fully understand, this parade is for him a necessity, an act of penance, as though this day has been set aside each spring to atone for all the sins that have gone before. When Charlie slips on that jacket, later this morning, he will no longer be father and husband, no longer a farmer immersed in the ordinary flow of things. He will step beyond all that—beyond her cognizance and reach. Off to some distant place. To another, more tortuous, time.

But for now he is still plain Charlie Holt, asleep. The father of this unknown child, unfolding within her belly somewhere. Almost as though he hears her thoughts, Charlie opens his eyes and with a sudden movement thrusts back the covers, though he does not immediately leap from bed, the way he often does. Instead, he turns and lays one hand upon her thigh.

"Hadn't we ought to get going?" she murmurs. "If we're to make it for your parade?"

"Oh, another few minutes won't matter, one way or the other," Charlie replies. "Good morning, you Rose of Sharon. Good morning, you wife of mine."

There are more people in town than she's ever seen before. Today, after the parade, a new monument is to be unveiled at the cemetery, in honor of all the martyred dead. They had to leave the wagon on the other side of the depot, on account of all the vehicles left beside the road.

Everywhere, women and children and Negroes are jammed along the street. The men are all down at the depot, trying to arrange themselves into lines, like they do every year. Even the younger men are there, those who were only boys when the fighting occurred.

She claims a spot in front of the hardware store, next to the street so the children can see, and searches the crowd for Sallie or Flora or anybody else she might know. Here and there she nods to a neighbor or friend, but most of the folks around her are strangers, from the opposite ends of the county, or maybe even the next county over. Some of the women wear mourning, and others have tied black ribbons to their bonnets or sleeves. She wishes she had thought to wear such a ribbon herself, in memory of Aaron. But would Charlie understand?

Aaron's name is never spoken between them, as though by tacit consent the past has been laid away. Charlie, she senses, does not like to be reminded of those early sweetheart years she shared with Aaron. He is jealous—and yet he still grieves for Aaron too.

The stores are open, and business is brisk, although most establishments bear hand-lettered signs to announce their closure when the parade begins. Vendors roam through the crowd, selling pinwheels and ginger cakes. It's an aggravation to have to keep telling the children no. She holds tightly to Jimmy-Jack, afraid of losing him in all this throng. The child won't stand still but leaps about, until her arm is half wrenched from its socket. All the children are excited.

"Look! There's Elijah!" Little Charles exclaims. "And, Mama, if *he* can go down to the depot by himself, then why can't I?"

She looks where Little Charles points, and sure enough, Elijah, Flora's boy, is waving from the opposite side of the street.

"Ya-hoo there, Elijah!" she hollers across to the boy. "Where's your mother?"

But Elijah merely shrugs.

"Please, Mama, can't I go?"

Ever since they arrived, Little Charles has pestered her to let him go down to the depot.

"Oh, all right," she says to him now. "I reckon you can go, providing you stick close to Elijah. And don't you bother your daddy. Lord knows how you'll ever find us again in all this crowd, but you know where the wagon's at, so don't keep us waiting, son."

Little Charles gives a whoop and dashes away, but she can't help calling after him:

"Son, watch where you're going, do you hear?"

The street's an unholy mess, worse than usual, from all the litter and manure. And the weather has turned out hot, which is no surprise—her face, her dress, her hands are already damp with perspiring. She wishes now she'd picked a spot on the opposite side of the street, where there's more shade, but it's too late now.

At the first sound of a drum, Jimmy-Jack bursts from her grip in a frenzy of joy, clapping his hands and jumping up and down. Even quiet Robbie is shouting and jumping. She grabs each boy by an overall strap and hangs on for dear life. The drums and bugles, still hidden from view, are playing a lively tune, as though this were a frolic or a dance, instead of a somber occasion to honor the fallen and the dead. Down the street, barely visible above the crowd, she can see the banners waving. But no flag. It would take unusual daring to march down this street waving the Stars and Bars. The Yankees would be right back here for sure.

And now the parade is directly upon them. Leading the way are the horsemen—officers probably, judging from all the braid—and then comes the makeshift band, and finally the men themselves, in long wavering lines, four abreast. Some are somber, gazing to neither left nor right, while others appear more jovial, calling out to family and friends. Hundreds of men, of every description: old and young, tall and short, fat and thin, some with beards and some without. They are clad in every conceivable kind of attire. Some have caps and some do not. Some wear jackets of gray but ordinary trousers, while for others it's the other way around. And a considerable number wear no uniform at all but are dressed as though hunting for possum or squirrel, their shotguns slung over their shoulders.

Almost every man in this county is out there marching today, even the halt and the lame. Some swing by on crutches, with empty trousers legs folded high, and many of the others have empty sleeves pinned to one side or another. She recognizes Thomas Barnes from down the road, and her sister Sallie's Will, and dozens of others, but she does not spot Charlie himself until Sophie calls out:

"Mama, look! There he is!"

Charlie is one of the somber ones. Though he inclines his head just slightly towards where they stand, his expression does not shift as he passes, keeping pace with the others. It is always rather a shock to have his lopsided gait brought to attention again.

She shudders, her heart beating faster than the drums. *Nothing in life can be taken for granted.* That is the message of this parade. She closes her eyes against this reminder, and when she opens them again, a mule-drawn wagon is passing so close that she could reach out and touch the iron-rimmed wheels. Huddled in that wagon are some of the most pathetic human creatures she's ever seen: young-old men with vacant stares, drooling, some of them. These were soldiers too, she suddenly realizes. Killed and destroyed, just as surely as if a bullet had actually pierced their hearts.

"And, look, Mama! Look a-there!" Sophie calls out again. "It's Little Charles!"

She turns from watching the wagon and gives her attention to the marching again. A line of boys is passing by, with Little Charles and Elijah in their midst. A shadow parade. The boys march in formation, some with sticks across their shoulders in raw imitation of the men. And immediately behind the white boys comes a cluster of colored ones, marching too. Ragged and barefoot, most of them, but not to be outdone.

Already the crowd is breaking apart, surging into the street and flowing towards the cemetery, where the speeches will soon begin. She herself does not move immediately but lifts one hand to adjust her sunbonnet and to wipe the dampness from her brow, and in that instant, that one half-second of release, the child Robbie darts into the moving throng and completely disappears.

It takes her another half-second to absorb the fact, and then to react. She yanks at Jimmy-Jack with one arm and grabs Sophie with her other hand, dragging the girl along as she starts to run, pushing her way through the crowd. Nowhere does she see the child. How could Robbie move so fast? Her bonnet slides off and into the street, trampled under foot, but she does not bother with that.

"Excuse me! Excuse me!" she cries, trying to move faster than the general flow.

People everywhere. Jimmy-Jack screams with fright, and she herself can scarcely breathe. Where can Robbie be? Has he vanished into the air? Has he already been smashed to death under foot? She catches up to the group of marching boys, only to find no Robbie among them. Little Charles and Elijah join her as the crowd surges around the corner at the Methodist church.

"It's Robbie!" she hoarsely shouts. "We've got to find him before he gets hurt or killed!"

Desperate, she searches the constantly shifting crowd, looking behind each woman's skirt, checking each child she sees, and at the same time trying to watch both sides of the street.

"Lord! Lord!" she cries, but takes no time to formulate a more specific prayer.

The throng rushes through the cemetery gates and along the gravel drive to where the new monument stands, a bronze soldier atop a granite block. The crowd begins to halt, spreading out in a circle.

And then she sees him.

Off to one side, away from the crowd, on a grassy stretch of tombstone-studded lawn that's shaded by a magnolia. Annie Jones, Henley and Josephine's girl, stands with the child, gripping his hand. Leading her gaggle of children, she hurries toward them. So out of breath that she cannot speak, she sets Jimmy-Jack, still crying, down upon the grass and reaches for the other child, the prodigal one. She clasps Robbie to her and weeps. The boy is covered with dirt, and one of his overall straps is torn, but he seems unharmed, blinking his eyes as calmly as though he were a hundred years old and had been to the moon and back. All-knowing, all-wise, and feeling no particular need to speak of his adventures. When she kisses his cheek, he rests his head on her shoulder for a moment, and then squirms to be set down.

"Annie," she turns to the girl, "where on earth did you find him?"

Annie could be no older than twelve, skinny and dark, her head wrapped in a pink-checked cloth.

"Oh, he just run me by," the girl replies, "somewheres back there a-ways, and I says to myself, Miz Lina don't want her youngun running off by hisself like that—so I just reached out and catched him, that's all. Our littlest boy, he be just like that, so I knows how it is."

Exhausted, she drops to the grass between the marble slabs and spreads her skirt for the little boys to sit on, one on either side, and Sophie sits down too. On the opposite slope, the ceremonies have begun, and she can hear a voice wafted high, something about the glory, about the honored dead.

The sun is down, and the little boys, bless them both, are already asleep, worn out from today's excitement. She stands at the back door, waiting her turn to wash up. It will take more than one basin of water to remove the dust and sweat accumulated this day. She would like to bathe from head to toe, except that she's much too tired to haul in the water for a tub.

On the porch, Charlie stands with his shirt off, his chest bare. The first thing Charlie did this afternoon, on reaching home again, was to change out of his uniform and back into farming clothes. Now he cups his hands into the basin and splashes his face, then gives his head a shake, scattering drops of water as he reaches for the flour sack that hangs by the door.

"Aren't those clouds a pretty sight?" he says, still holding the towel.

To the west, a pair of low clouds bear a ruddy reflection of light. Above them, barely visible, is a thin sliver of moon. Perhaps it's a sign. Immediately she thinks of the child inside her, still as fragile as that pale infant moon.

"Charlie," she says, "I believe I'm expecting again."

Charlie grins. He hooks the towel on its nail and turns to put both hands on her shoulders. Gently he kisses her, his beard damp, his skin smelling of soap.

"Miss Lina, my sweet honey," he says, "there's nothing makes me as happy as news like that!"

Shamelessly, right on the porch, he lifts her dress and petticoat and feels her abdomen, running his hand over the curve of her belly, as though to verify the child within.

"A daughter or a son?" he asks, letting her skirt fall clear again.

"A daughter, I do hope—but more than likely another son."

"Well, we can't name him Robert E. Lee," Charlie muses, "because we've already got one of those, and Stonewall Jackson's been honored too. But we've got plenty of time to give the matter some thought."

"I *have* been thinking," she says, her voice low as she searches Charlie's face. "If it's a boy, I want to name him Aaron."

Charlie does not react the way she expected; he does not frown or turn away.

"You're absolutely right," he says, pulling her close again. "We'll name him Aaron. It's time we got used to hearing that name again."

Chapter 19

November 1878

This is her sixth time around, and by now she ought to be used to walking with her feet splayed out, leaning slightly backward to compensate for the bulk in front...to having her belly swollen almost to bursting, while everything else—heart, stomach, lungs—has been shoved aside to make room for this intruder, who kicks her awake every night...to this constant fatigue. All she really wants is to lie in bed and sleep for several hours straight. Somehow, this past day or two, the whole business has become an intolerable burden. Fortunately the end is just a few weeks away.

Her abdomen presses against the table edge as she smoothes out a length of blue chambray and weights down the pattern pieces. For Christmas she is making Charlie a new shirt. Cutting out a garment is always tedious, but it's far more tiresome now, when every move is distorted. At least when she gets to the stitching, she can sit down and prop up her feet.

About midway each pregnancy, she decides that carrying a child is a physical pleasure, but by the final stretch, she is anxious to have it over with, to reclaim her bodily organs for their normal uses again—although she is scarcely certain which *is* normal: fallowness or this.

The scissors still in her hand, she crosses to the calendar beside the back door. Today is November twenty-ninth, with five or six weeks to go, according to her best calculation. She hopes to carry *this* child full term, if she possibly can. Not like poor Lydia Mary—but she'd better not ponder that. All these past months, she has done her best *not* to remember. Even so, she can't help but acknowledge her fear. *What if it should happen again?* She has never spoken of this to Charlie, though. Some apprehensions are better left unsaid. All she can do is hope and pray—and wait.

But waiting doesn't get shirts made. She'd better take advantage of this quiet, before Sophie and Little Charles come home from school, or the little boys get tired of playing outside.

She has cut out the collar and sleeves and is starting on the yoke when she hears Charlie's tread on the porch, though he does not come inside immediately. He has been clearing cornstalks, but when he opens the door, his face and hands are clean, and his hair has been slicked into place. Charlie crosses to the front room, and in a moment reappears. Under his arm is the geography book that Miss Beatrice Campbell lent him the other day. At the back door, his hand on the knob, he turns around.

"I believe I'll run over to the schoolhouse," he says, "and take them a load of firewood."

Her heart lurches—or was it the child?

"If you hurry," she replies, trying to speak in an even tone, "you'll be there before Sophie and Little Charles depart. And if I know those two, they'll be glad for a ride back home."

"Oh, I expect I'll be there a right good while. Stacking and such. There's no call for the children to stay hanging around."

"Little Charles could help you stack."

"Little Charles has chores to do at home."

With that, he opens the door and is gone. From the front window she watches the wagon pull into the road. There is no firewood visible from here. Charlie does not even glance towards the house as he rolls past. The afternoon is sunny, but nothing offers the slightest reassurance—not the dead brown weeds of the roadside, nor the abandoned stalks of the field across the way.

She flings her scissors on the table. In the front room, she climbs onto the bed. She lies on her back, hands clasped over the calico slope of her abdomen, her eyes filling with tears.

Are there no other men who can split cordwood besides Charlie Holt? This is the second time this week that Charlie has carried a load to the school. Altogether, since school reopened and Miss Campbell reappeared, he has been to the schoolhouse a dozen times for one thing or another—putting new pegs in the cloakroom, or fixing the steps. Miss Campbell, of course, is always there, and lately she's been lending Charlie books. He sits up half the night, reading them through, so he'll have an excuse to return them again.

What can she do? She is thirty-four, a shapeless mess, chained to this huge abdomen and not at liberty to come and go, like some folks do. And she doesn't have time to read books. Miss Beatrice Campbell is fresh and young and wears bright frocks instead of a faded tent that has seen many seasons of wear. She hates Miss Beatrice Campbell— hates her with all her heart.

And now that she reflects upon it, she hates Charlie too. It will serve him right if she dies when this baby comes. But would he even care? Then he'd be free to marry Miss Campbell and bring her here to live. Sophie and Little Charles would probably like that too. Then everyone could sit around and talk about mountain ranges and South

America, while she lies moldering in her grave, useless and forgotten.

She is crying so hard that she does not hear the back door open or the little boys come in, until Robbie and Jimmy-Jack stand beside the bed, their eyes wide with alarm. Before she can send them back outside, they climb onto the bed, and both start crying too. She wraps an arm around each child and sobs all the harder.

"Who in tarnation left this door standing open? Haven't I told you folks about that?"

Did she fall asleep? She nudges the children aside and struggles to rise. Her dress is every which way, and her hair has come loose. She needs to blow her nose but has no handkerchief. She swings her legs over the edge of the bed just as Charlie comes into the room, with Sophie and Little Charles right behind.

"Mama!" Sophie exclaims, and darts across the room. "Is it the baby? Is it like that other time?"

She shakes her head, not trusting herself to speak.

"There appeared to be a sufficiency of firewood on hand," Charlie announces, "so I came back home."

Why did he change his mind? Wasn't Miss Campbell there today? Weren't there any more books to lend? Charlie steps aside to let her pass as she moves to the kitchen, where she gathers up her scissors and folds the chambray cloth. She does not feel up to any more cutting today.

"Little Charles," Charlie speaks sharply to the boy, who lurks in a corner, "haven't I told you to keep this stovebox full? Well, then, get busy! And, Sophie, don't you have some chores to do?"

Charlie jams his hat back on and steps to the door.

"Lina," he turns around to say, "I'll do the milking to-night and see to the chickens, so you can rest yourself some more."

But chores are sometimes a comfort. The yard is in shadow, and the chill of evening is in the air when she wraps her shawl close and steps outside. The wagon stands beside the barn, and she cannot help but pass it. She peers between the slats. Yes, there *is* firewood piled in there, already split—but only enough for one or two days.

When she goes into the barn to fetch a pan of cracked corn, she is distressed to find Charlie sitting there, shucking a few ears more. She almost turns away but does not. She does not look at Charlie, does not acknowledge his presence as she bends over the barrel to scoop out a ration of feed.

"Lina, I *told* you I would do the chickens," Charlie says.

"I'm not so useless yet but what I can't see to my own hens!" she snaps back in reply. "So there's no need to trouble yourself about *me!*"

But her voice betrays her and ends in a quaver. She refuses to look at Charlie, but she hears him suck in his breath. He stands up.

"Lina, you sit yourself down right here!" he says, pointing to the overturned box he has just vacated. "We're going to have ourselves a talk, right now, before this business goes any further—even if I'm not entirely sure what there is to say."

She hasn't the strength to resist. But is she going to cry again? Averting her eyes, she lowers herself onto the carton and holds her abdomen, as though to shield the child from Charlie.

"And the reason I'm not entirely sure what there is to say," Charlie continues, "is because I'm not entirely sure what it is that's wrong—though I suspect it has to do with the fact that I was over to the schoolhouse this afternoon."

"I can leave!" she blurts out, unable to control herself. "I'll pack up and leave, if that's what you want! I'll find myself someplace else to stay! Just as soon as I've borne this child!"

"I thought so," Charlie mutters. "I *thought* it was that— and maybe you're right."

He sits on a keg directly opposite. Their knees almost touch, though she still does not look up.

"Lina, I have been sinning against you."

Her head flies up. She starts to rise, but her legs fail, and she has to sit down again.

"Oh, I've not gone so far as to compromise Miss Campbell's honor!" Charlie says. "Thank goodness, it's not worked around to *that!* Not yet, at any rate. But if it's sinning just to look at a woman that way—and the Lord was mighty specific about that point—if it's sinning to have such thoughts in your mind, then I must confess that I have truly been sinning."

She is silent.

"Miss Campbell is a pretty young woman. And she's considerably smart in the head, too."

She does not speak.

"It's not that I'm dissatisfied here to home, Lina, or bored either—fact is, it doesn't have anything to do with *you* at all. It's just that sometimes I start imagining what my life would be like if things were different, if I lived someplace else entirely, or in a different time—or with somebody else."

She does not reply.

"Lina, I don't know if you understand what I mean, what I'm trying to say—though I expect you've done *your* share of imagining how it would be, married to someone else."

"That's different!" she shoots back. "He's *dead,* and you know it! Besides, that was a long time ago!"

She will not listen to any more. She musters all her strength and manages to stand, but Charlie stands too, and he blocks her way.

"Well, go and sin no more!" he exclaims. "The Lord said that too, as I recall, and that's *exactly* what I intend. So I'm asking you to forgive me, Lina—and if you can't do that, then at least I want you to understand me on that point. I reckon other folks can tend to the schoolhouse for a while."

Now she *is* starting to cry, but she bites her lip to stave the flow. Instantly Charlie takes hold of her arms, trying to pull her close, but her abdomen gets in the way.

"Lina, please believe me!" he says. "Miss Beatrice Campbell is a buttercup, a pretty flower that blooms in the spring. But *you*—well, you are my meat and potatoes! I love you, Miss Lina! I *need* you! I most earnestly do."

She bursts out crying in full, and it is Charlie who wipes the tears away, who arranges her shawl again. His arm around her, he leads her from the barn.

"I declare, though," he says, as they step into the yard, "but it will be a considerable relief when this child is here, so that you and me, Miss Lina, can resume our regular sparking again."

Chapter 20

Christmas Eve, 1878

When will Santa Claus get here, Jimmy-Jack wants to know. And how can he come, if there's no snow? It's the fourth time he's asked her this morning. The child is so keyed up that it wouldn't take much for him to fly through the air himself. This is the first year he has been able to remember the Christmas before.

And she herself is as bad as the boy, only it's not Christmas that she's waiting for. Wouldn't it be something, if the child should arrive tonight, on Christmas Eve? All morning she has been thinking about the Virgin Mary, as swollen as she herself is now, riding along on the back of a mule, on a winter day just like this. Riding along, with the pains coming on, sharp and strong, and no place to lie down except in some stranger's drafty barn. No midwife either—only Joseph, and him probably without the least notion of what to do.

She returns her attention to the egg whites she is beating into glossy peaks.

"Jimmy-Jack, here's your snow!" she says to the child, holding the bowl low for him to see. "Up yonder where the Yankees live, it looks like this all winter long."

Jimmy-Jack climbs into a chair to watch as she folds the whites into her batter. She fills two of the tins and holds a portion aside for the middle layer, to be darkened with nutmeg and raisins. Japanese fruitcake, this is called. She has never met anyone who's actually been to Japan, but if she ever does, she intends to ask whether they make their cakes this way, and do they serve it for Christmas too?

"Sophie, I need your help," she calls up the attic stairs.

What did the Virgin Mary do, without a daughter to help with oven doors and all the other things that require a body to stoop and bend?

She is washing the bowls and the mixing spoon when Charlie comes into the kitchen, his cheeks red from the cold.

"Lina, get your shawl, and maybe even two—it's right nippy out. I need you to step outside with me for a while. There's a little matter I want you to superintend."

"And I expect I don't even need to ask what it is," she says, drying her hands and calling to Sophie again, to mind the cake while she's gone.

Outside, she pulls her shawls tighter against the bitter cold. At the barn, Charlie picks up his ax, and they set out, Charlie leading the way, walking slow to accommodate her waddling gait. Lord, but she must look like the Queen of Sheba now, sallying forth with all her veils and train! They pass through the orchard, where the ground is frozen, the trees all leafless.

"Now remember," she says, "I want a tree that's considerably smaller than the one last year. The house is crowded enough as it is, and with company tomorrow, there's scarcely room for us all to stand, much less sit down to eat."

"You can judge for yourself," Charlie says. "That's why I brought you along."

Charlie is as wild about Christmas as any child. He never lets Christmas go by without putting up a tree, the larger the better, and he has whittled an entire collection of wooden stars and bells, to be hung on the branches with scraps of red ribbon and yarn.

"Charlie, do you have a particular tree in mind—or should we be keeping an eye out as we go along?"

"You'll see," he says.

They enter the woods. Much of their land remains uncleared, although Charlie has chopped away at it year after year. When they reach the place where Aaron's house would have been, she stops in surprise. The entire space between the two large oaks has been cleared of brush and lesser trees—except for one small cedar, right in the middle, decked out in a dozen red bows.

"Charlie, that tree is just perfect!" she exclaims.

And then she realizes that the ground around the cedar has been leveled and smoothed, with stakes and string marking a large enclosure. In each corner stands a brick column, two or three feet tall.

"Charles Wesley Holt, would you please tell me what this is all about?"

"It's a house, Lina—can't you tell? It's the beginnings of a house that I'm building. This is your Christmas present, Miss Lina."

She is stunned and does not know what to say. Charlie puts down his ax and takes her by the arm.

"Course, scripture says to build your house on a rock," he says, "but I couldn't find sufficient rocks just lying around, so I had to make do with brick. I hired Henley Jones to put these pillars up—fact is, he finished just yesterday evening."

He helps her step over the string, and they turn to face in the general direction of the road, still hidden by a strip of trees.

"Here's the front room," he says, with a sweep of his arm, "and that's the dining room—I'm building you a separate room just for eating. And back there is your kitchen.

And one of the bedrooms will be over yonder, across the hall."

She turns to look where he points, towards the cedar tree.

"I'd take you upstairs," Charlie says, "and show you the other bedrooms, except that the stairs aren't in working order yet."

"You mean it's a *two*-story house?"

"Why, certainly, Miss Lina," Charlie replies. "I'm building you the fanciest house I can."

Standing behind her, he wraps his arms around her middle. She shivers at the touch of his beard, icy cold against her neck, but is glad for the warmth of his body.

"I declare but I'm overwhelmed!" she says, leaning back against him. "It's a wonderful house, and a wonderful present. But where's the money coming from? I thought you said this year's cotton didn't bring but...."

"It didn't," he interrupts. "But I've decided to sell off that stand of timber across the road—I want to start farming that section anyhow. And then once we're settled in here, I'll cash-rent the other place, and that'll help some. The way I figure, it won't take but three or four years before we've worked our way back to the clear again."

Money is Charlie's domain, aside from the pennies her eggs bring in.

"But, Charlie," she says, "isn't it a terrible risk, taking on the building of a house like this?"

"Well, of course it's a risk," he answers, stepping aside to pick up his ax again. "But raising crops is a risk, and having a baby's a risk—can you tell me anything in life that's *not* a risk? But sometimes you reach a point where you have to decide whether you're going to try and leap ahead, or whether you're going to just keep poking along the same old row. So two or three weeks ago, I decided that I'm not getting any younger, and now's the time."

He crosses to the cedar and takes a swing. The little tree shudders with the impact of the ax.

"Besides," Charlie says, straightening up again, "I want to make sufficient room for this next son of mine. And I expect there'll be more children coming along before *we're* through, Miss Lina, you and me."

He resumes his work with the ax until the tree is down. One of the ribbons falls off as he shoulders the cedar, but she cannot stoop to retrieve it.

"Well, Charlie Holt, you can't fool me!" she says, laughing as she tries to keep up. "I know *exactly* why you want a bigger house—it's so next year you can have an *enormous* Christmas tree, ten feet tall and ten feet across, at least. Now, tell me the truth—isn't that why?"

"Yep," Charlie says, bobbing ahead with his load. "Miss Lina, my sweet honey, I admit it—I already thought of that."

Chapter 21

New Year's Eve, 1878

Drowsily, she watches the large white flakes come down, though from here in the bed she cannot see if they melt when they reach the ground. But the tiny one needn't worry about staying warm, because it's snug enough in this room—hot even, from the blazing fire that Charlie built. Gently she lifts the wrapped-up bundle beside her and studies the baby's face, with his mouth, even in sleep, puckered as though to suck.

This child's arrival, about quarter past noon, went much easier than any of the others, and Aunt Essie has already been carried back home, which is a good thing, because with this snow there's no telling how long the roads will last. Charlie has gone now to fetch the children before it gets any worse.

She can hear her mama in the kitchen, preparing supper. Thank goodness for Mama, who came Christmas Day and has stayed ever since. Despite the work, Mama seems to enjoy these visits—for the change of scenery as much as anything, she suspects.

The smell of ham catches her attention. She is hungry, she suddenly realizes. As a matter of fact, she is absolutely starving. Why, she could eat half a ham right now—or even just a bowl of cowpeas—but she'd better have *something* soon, before she grows any weaker. She doesn't believe she can wait until suppertime. She starts to get out of bed but quickly discovers the foolishness of that and leans against the pillows once more.

"Mama?" she sheepishly calls.

With all the noise from the kitchen, she gets no reply. Mama doesn't hear as keenly as she used to. She ought to be ashamed of herself, to lie here and squawk like a child, but the hunger is growing intense.

"Mama?" she calls again, a little louder.

Mama appears in the doorway, wiping her hands on her apron, her face flushed from the stove.

"Daughter, was that you hollering?"

"It was, I'm ashamed to say. I reckon I'm a little mite hungry."

"Law me, but I expect you are!" Mama exclaims. "At dinnertime, you were busy with other occupations, as I recall. Well, I'll fry you an egg right quick, to tide you over until my biscuits are done."

Mama crosses to add more wood to the fire and then leans over the bed to view the child.

"Still sleeping?" Mama asks. "My, but he's a sweet little thing."

She is propped up in bed, holding the child with one arm and with the other hand attempting to feed herself, when she hears the wagon roll into the yard. In a moment more, all four children come clattering in, their faces bright, the snowflakes not yet dissolved from their scarves and hair. They ignore their grandmother's efforts to slow them down and immediately rush to the bed.

"Daddy says it's a *boy!*" Sophie confronts her immediately. "Well, I want to know how come! I've been praying for a *sister* for weeks now, so how come we get this boy?"

"I don't know," she answers the girl. "But we have to assume that the Lord Almighty knows what He's doing."

The baby has fallen asleep again. Gently she removes her breast from his mouth and holds out the infant for the children to see. Jimmy-Jack starts to climb onto the bed—coat, shoes, and all—but Charlie lifts the boy away and swings him high, over his head. Jimmy-Jack bursts out crying, and as soon as his feet touch the floor, he runs off to the kitchen.

"Well, children, what do you think?" Charlie asks the ones who remain. "I expect it won't be long before this new one is out in the fields to help us grass the cotton. He's near-bout big enough right now, it appears to me."

The children do not laugh.

"What's the matter, Robbie?" Charlie says, chucking the boy's chin. "Do you think he'll have to wait for a little while longer? Do you think he's still too small?"

Solemnly Robbie nods.

"Well, I know one thing," she says. "It doesn't take a baby long to learn how to wet his britches—they're born with that knowledge, I've found. Sophie, hand me one of those diapers stacked over yonder on the chest."

For health and strength...and especially for the safe delivery of this child...for food, shelter, and warmth...for sunshine, flowers, and Christmas trees.... As she sits up in bed and nurses the child, she tries to list in her mind all the past year's blessings. She is not praying exactly—her thoughts are too diffuse for that—but she does not want this year to expire without acknowledging her gratitude.

Charlie comes in from the porch, his last trip outside for the night, and with him brings a blast of frosty air, so that she lifts the quilt to shield the child from draft.

"Still snowing?" she asks.

"Pretty good," Charlie replies, hanging his coat on the peg and crossing to the hearth to warm his hands. "I expect there'll be enough white by morning for the children to have some fun. I don't know which excited them more—the snow, or that little one there. It's been quite a day."

He comes to the bed and lays a cold hand against her cheek. The room is still except for the crack of a log. The lamp casts a yellow glow over the child in her arms, over Charlie and herself. But the baby begins to cry as she wraps him up tight for the night, a familiar piercing bleat that cuts through the quiet.

"Here, hand him to me," Charlie says. "Let me hold this son of mine."

Charlie picks up the child and rests the bundle against his shoulder, patting the rounded hump. In a moment the child is quiet again. There's a catch in her throat at the sight of Charlie, with his beard and his large rough hands, holding such a fragile mite. The baby's small round head is nestled in the crook of his neck. She loves Charlie most acutely at moments like these.

"Well, I expect we'll hear from him again before this night is through," Charlie whispers as he hands her the baby, fast asleep.

"We ought to record his birth," she answers. "I'd like to do that now."

Charlie brings her the Bible, a bottle of ink, and the pen that Sophie uses for school. He adjusts the lamp so that the light falls more directly across the bed as she opens the Bible on her lap.

"Charlie," she says, looking up, before she dips the pen, "it *is* still Aaron, isn't it? You haven't changed your mind?"

"I thought we already agreed about that," he says, his hand on her shoulder. "But whether it's Aaron Thomas or Aaron Franklin—that's for you to decide."

Aaron Franklin Holt, born on this day, December 31, 1878, quarter past noon.... She writes in careful letters across the page, having to dip the pen again before she's through.

She lifts the book and blows until she can no longer discern a gleam upon the words.

"There," she says, closing the Bible and handing it back to Charlie. "I just hope *this* Aaron Holt gets a chance to live a full life—*and* to know the sweet pleasure of having his own children too."

"Amen!" Charlie replies. "For sure, I say amen to that!"

Part Three

Death in the Midst of Life

Chapter 22

October 1887

She lays the baby Sparta on the bed, with a pad underneath in case of accident.

"Sparta Sue, I love you...," she croons as she holds the child with one hand. The baby responds with a happy, boisterous kick.

Downstairs, she can hear a clatter as Sophie washes the noon dishes in great haste. Sophie dislikes all kitchen chores immensely, but give her a needle and some cloth, and she'll work for hours on end. Every dime the girl receives goes for fabric. Sophie has gotten far more use from the sewing machine that Charlie bought two crops ago than she herself ever has.

When Miss Sophie Holt gets married, she'll have plenty of quilts to carry with her—there's already a dozen pieced tops in the trunk, with the girl only fifteen and not even courting yet. It won't be long, though, unless Charlie pitches a fit. Sophie is still his favored-most child, and he doesn't take kindly to having young fellows come sniffing around. He was clearly peeved that one of Little Charles' friends was here last Sunday. There might have been a

143

scene, except that Sophie made a great show of paying the fellow no mind.

Sophie is clever and pert, and she has turned out fetching, with eyes that are blue like Charlie's but hair that's lighter than his. She is slender and tall. It's rather a shock to have your own children stand higher than you do yourself. Little Charles is equal to his daddy, in height at least, and Robbie and Jimmy-Jack are catching up.

One crop of children is nearly grown, but new ones are taking their place. She lifts the baby Sparta from the bed and pulls the rocking chair close to the window. She unbuttons her dress and begins to nurse the child, rocking slightly and singing a lullaby. Through the window she sees a cardinal sitting on a branch of the oak, a bright flash of red, with his mate beside him, in more sober hues. She never tires of looking out to this tree, its leaves now beginning to turn. It was her idea to take this upstairs room for Charlie and herself, in part to be closer to the children but in part for the view of this tree. Charlie had originally planned for them to sleep in the bedroom directly below, the one now occupied by Little Charles.

The child in her arms is almost asleep when Sophie calls up the stairs.

"Mama! Someone's turning in!"

Hastily she lays Sparta in the crib and buttons her dress again. She tries to smooth her hair as she hurries downstairs to the front porch.

A stranger is alighting from his buggy. He's a farmer, from the looks of him, dressed in clean overalls and with a straw hat on his head, which he removes at first sight of her. She doesn't recall having seen this gentleman before.

"Howdy, ma'am," the stranger says, coming to the base of the steps. "My name is Sparrow Jones, and I've been spending the past few days talking to folks hereabouts. I wonder is your husband to home? If he's out in the fields, maybe you could point me in the right direction, and I could speak to him there."

"Did your daddy already go back to his picking?" she asks Sophie, who stands behind her, holding the screen door open.

"Yes, ma'am."

Sometimes on the hottest days, Charlie stretches out on the floor of this porch to rest for a bit after dinner, but with the days growing shorter now, he won't spare even those few minutes but presses straight out to the field, especially at picking time. Charlie pushes himself so hard that she worries about him.

"Well, I expect you'd better go fetch him," she says to Sophie. "The boys can keep on picking while he comes to see what this gentleman wants.

At her insistence, Sparrow Jones takes a seat, though he declines a chair in favor of the top step, while she settles into the swing at the end of the porch. He hails from Texas, he tells her, and has a wife and three children that he misses a heap, having been on the road the past four weeks.

At last Charlie appears, tramping through the house and out the front door to shake the stranger's hand. She rises to leave, but Sparrow Jones insists he would be obliged if she could stay and listen too, since what he wants to discuss applies to womenfolk too, not just to men. She takes her seat again, rolling her hands in her apron and wishing she had her mending here.

"I've come up here to North Carolina," Sparrow Jones begins, "because I've been authorized to speak for a bunch of folks who call themselves the National Farmers' Alliance. We're plain dirt farmers, the same as you appear to be."

There's a light of recognition in Charlie's eye.

"Yes, I've been hearing about you Alliance folks," Charlie says. "I've been reading right much about you, and I knew you-all were moving into this state. Fact is, I've been wondering when your Alliance would work its way to here."

"Well, then, you probably know about the success we're having," Sparrow Jones says. "We're springing up faster than weeds in a cotton patch. Why, I personally, Sparrow H. Jones, have organized a half dozen groups, just in the past month. But let me ask you folks a question. What do you raise on this place? Cotton?"

"Well, mostly," Charlie replies. "That's the big one. We still call it our cash crop, even if it doesn't produce any cash. And then I generally raise yams and melons and a few other things. I sold three wagonloads of melons this summer, for shipping up north somewhere, and I probably cleared more on those melons than I will from half my cotton, if it's like last year again."

If it *is* like last year, a heap of folks will find themselves in a fix again. Ten years ago, a pound of cotton sold for twelve cents, but last fall it brought only seven. It costs almost that to raise it, when you count in the seed and the ginning. Charlie has not yet carried any of this year's crop to town, but word's going around that cotton is still on a downhill tilt. Well, it's been sliding so long that it ought to have reached the bottom by now, and be heading back up again. Isn't that how nature works? Barren one year, but fruitful the next? Seven lean cows, but seven fat ones too.

"Let me ask you something else," Sparrow Jones presses on. "Do you *own* this here place?"

"Yes, we do," Charlie replies. "Free and clear—and I intend to keep it that way."

"Well, even so, are you in any way beholden to a furnishing man? Down Texas, at any rate, most everybody has to get furnished in one form or another, just to have seeds to put in the ground. And the way things are rigged, as I'm sure you know, once you start getting furnished, it seems like you can never get free again. Is it like that around here?"

146

"Yes, here too," Charlie says. "Though *we* are not beholden, and thank the Lord we are not! When it comes to the point that I have to get furnished, then I'll plumb give up planting cotton—I've already decided that. Fact is, the reason I took up melons and yams is so if cotton fails, then at least we won't starve, even if we *do* have to go around half-clothed. My wife hasn't had to dress us in fig leaves yet, but I expect she could learn—we got some fig bushes over yonder."

She believes that Charlie would cut off his other leg if it would keep him out of debt. Never again. It took nearly eight years of worry to pay off the note on this house, what with cotton falling and the cash renter unable to pay a cent one year. Charlie let him stay on for another whole season, and finally settled for labor instead of cash. Now there's a good example of owing your shirt to the furnishing man, but there was no other way apparently. Every direction you look, it's the same for a lot of folks.

They have been fortunate so far, but it hasn't been easy. Five years ago, when the crop brought nothing in, Charlie announced one morning that he'd given up drinking coffee and was giving up light bread too—that she needn't buy any more coffee or flour on his account. Naturally the rest of them followed suit. It became a challenge, in fact, to see what she could devise, just using the fixings at hand. Indian puddings and assorted cornmeal cakes. It's amazing what folks can do, when they put their mind to it.

"We've seen some right hard times around these parts," Charlie says. "You can ask most anyone."

"I have been," Sparrow Jones replies. "That's why the Alliance sent me here—to talk to folks. But let me ask you one more question, Brother Holt, if you don't mind. Isn't it time us poor farmers get ourselves together and *do* something about the way things are? About how we're robbed and squeezed by the furnishing men, the banks, the railroads, and everybody else under the sun?"

"Amen to that!" Charlie says. "It's long past time, in fact. But what do you propose we do?"

"I propose you come to the meeting I'm setting up Saturday afternoon, over to the schoolhouse," Sparrow Jones says. "That's day after tomorrow, and be sure to bring the missus along—we need all the folks we can get."

"We'll be there," Charlie asserts. "You can count on it. And in the meantime, I'll see what I can do to pass the word along."

Charlie walks Sparrow Jones to his rig and watches him depart. When he returns to the porch, there's a grin on his face. To her surprise, he pulls her up and clasps his hands around her waist—and gives her a kiss, right in broad daylight.

"Well, Miss Lina, what do you think?" he says. "These are the folks I've been telling you about. This is hopeful news, Miss Lina! Well, I expect *this* is a day we'll remember for a right long while!"

Chapter 23

November 1887

NATIONAL FARMERS' ALLIANCE! The words wave like a banner over all their doings now, unfurling in the middle of nearly every conversation they've had at this table since that first meeting was held, a month ago.

"But, daughter, if you'd look over yonder to that calendar, you'd *see* that tomorrow is Alliance day," Charlie is saying to Sophie. "And don't you think that the future of this family—*and* the future of this state—is of greater consequence than going to town to buy frippery?"

"But, Daddy!" Sophie shoots right back. "If you'd look over yonder at that calendar, you'd *also* see that Christmas is only four weeks away, and there's a few notions that I need right now, so I can proceed with one or two matters that I have in mind. Besides, you're the one always saying it's more blessed to give than to receive. Well, if I don't get to town pretty soon, I won't be *able* to give, and certain other folks won't be able to receive!"

Charlie chuckles in spite of himself as he helps himself to sausage. If there's anyone in this family who can equal Charlie's quickness with words, it's Sophie. Still, no amount of wit could possibly deflect Charlie Holt from attending even the smallest gathering of the Clearwater Branch, National Farmers' Alliance—and Sophie ought to know that by now.

But Sophie does have a point about Christmas.

"I can stay home tomorrow," she interjects. "I can stay home with the children myself, and then Sophie and Little Charles can take the wagon to town. They can drop you off at the schoolhouse, Charlie, before they go. I expect Thomas Barnes would give you a ride back home, once the meeting's over."

Charlie flashes her a look of hurt astonishment.

"Lina, have you *forgot?* It's the election tomorrow, and we want everybody there. Aren't you planning to vote?"

"Why, I hadn't thought," she says. "I reckon I just assumed it was something you menfolks would do."

"But, Sister Holt, aren't you a sworn-in member? And Little Charles too?"

"Yes, I reckon so."

"Well, all right, then," Charlie says. "Here's what we'll do. First thing in the morning, we'll make a quick trip to town—all of us—so you womenfolk can get your trading done. And then we'll stop back to home and leave Sophie and the children off. And *then* we'll get on to the meeting. Now, does everybody here agree to that? If so, will you all say 'aye'?"

A chorus of "ayes" sounds around the table. Even two-year-old Ida chimes in, although the child doesn't have the least idea what the discussion is about.

"Do I hear any 'nays'?"

Silence. No one dissents.

"Well, then," Charlie says. "It appears to me that the preceding motion is carried unanimously. Now, do I hear a motion that we get on with the business of eating this meal?"

He winks at Aaron, to his left.

"I move it!" Aaron says, eagerly raising his hand.

"Brother Aaron Franklin Holt has moved that we get on with our eating," Charlie states. "Do I hear a second?"

"Me! Daddy, let me!" six-year-old Jeffrey insists.

"Brother Thomas Jefferson Holt has seconded the motion," Charlie says. "Now will somebody kindly pass those turnip greens down this way?"

The room hums with talk. There must be sixty people here—three times as many as when this thing began. Sparrow Jones was certainly right about weeds in a cotton patch. She's never seen anything like it. There hasn't been such excitement around these parts since Lord knows when. Certainly not since they built this schoolhouse they're sitting in—although not everyone *is* sitting, since half the men are standing at the back of the room.

She threads her needle and begins to sew a patch onto the seat of Jimmy-Jack's overalls as Will Johnson goes to the front and signals for quiet. Will has been serving as a temporary chairman these past few weeks, but some folks contend that he should be prohibited from running for permanent office, since his brother-in-law, the other end of the county, has a store and furnishes Negro croppers. People say that in a pinch Will is liable to side with the bankers. But other folks say that Will Johnson raises cotton too, and if he's not a farmer, then what is he? Besides, they say, the Alliance *needs* men like Will who know their way around. Charlie has written to the Alliance headquarters at Raleigh for a judgment on the matter but hasn't got an answer yet. In the meantime, Will continues to call the meetings to order.

The first item of business is to initiate all newcomers, because anyone who's not officially sworn in will have to leave. The rules are perfectly clear about that. The welcome mat is out for any farmer who pledges to work for the cause, but that welcome doesn't apply to enemies or spies.

By the time Will Johnson has been confirmed as president, she is starting on a second patch. The vice president, doorkeeper, and chaplain are all chosen. They are working their way down the list.

"All right, we've come to secretary," Will Johnson announces. "Do I hear any names?"

Jeffrey tore his shirt last week while climbing a pecan tree. Little boys are rough on clothes. She pins the square of gingham in place, folding under each raw edge.

"Sister Lina Holt!" someone shouts from the rear of the room.

She gives a start, pricking herself and snarling her thread as well.

"No, sir, he doesn't mean *me*! It's a mistake!" she tries to call out, but her voice sounds like a stranger's and won't cooperate. She is not used to speaking in front of people this way, and Will appears not to hear.

But who ever heard of a *woman* doing such a thing? A respectable married woman, a mother—and forty-four years old at that? Are people snickering? She's too embarrassed to turn around and look, and Will Johnson is already scrawling her name onto the blackboard.

"Excuse me, but I just can't possibly...." She tries to speak again, louder this time, and succeeds at last in catching Will Johnson's attention.

"Oh, yes you can, Sister Holt! You can do it!" a man's voice calls from the back of the room. "We're absolute certain you can!"

It was Thomas Barnes, then, who got her into this. Shame on him. Or did Charlie put him up to such a trick? She wouldn't put it past Charlie to try such a crazy move. He's wrong, though—he's plumb-out wrong, and when they're home again, she'll tell him so. Why, look, her hands are trembling so much that she can't even sew on a decent patch. She folds her mending and puts it away in the basket at her feet. She wishes she'd never come today.

Pressing her hands together, she tries to shape a prayer: *Lord, Lord, if it be Thy will....* There's a moment of relief when Rosemary Hennings' name is written below her own, but immediately the voting begins. She closes her eyes so that she won't see the hands being raised and holds her breath, listening to the painful screech of chalk against the board. Did Jesus tremble so as He prayed in Gethsemane?

"Well, it looks like Sister Holt is our new secretary," Will Johnson announces at last.

So be it. She opens her eyes.

"What is it you want me to do?" she asks. "Somebody's got to explain, because I'm just a married woman and haven't got the slightest notion what you want me to do."

"Well, come on up and sit right here," Will Johnson says, pulling out the teacher's chair.

She obeys, smoothing her skirt beneath her but keeping her eyes to the floor to avoid seeing the crowd in the room. If she thinks about the sixty people here, and herself in front of them all, she will never be able to do it.

"And here," Will Johnson says, reaching into the teacher's desk for a pencil and a pad of ruled paper. "Write down everything we say and everything we do. And when we get the treasurer chosen, we'll issue you a dime to buy a notebook to keep our records in."

Slowly she writes across the top of the pad: *Voting Day, Clearwater Branch.* It's awkward shaping the words. Her fingers are stiff, and her hand objects.

"I'm not used to it yet," she says, "but if you folks insist, then I'm obliged to try."

"That's my woman! Now isn't she something?"

This time it *is* Charlie who calls out, but she dares not look at him.

"Lina, I knew all along you could do it!" he says. "It may seem hard at first—but I expect everyone here is getting used to doing things that we've never done before!"

Chapter 24

January 1888

Brunswick stew, spicy with turnips and thick with lima beans, the way Sophie likes it best. There's cornbread of course, and a salad of apples, raisins, and pecans. Even the cake is Sophie's favorite, made from a dozen eggs and with the peel of a lemon grated into slivers. She is worried, though, that the cake won't taste sweet, because she lacked a quarter-cup having enough sugar. Charlie won't let her buy any sugar until the new Alliance Exchange opens for business in another month of two.

In the meantime, he suggests that they take any money that *might* have been spent on sugar and purchase another share in the Exchange itself. Charlie has already bought six shares, and he keeps the certificates between the pages of the Bible, marking the parable of the talents. He says they're bound to save money when they can trade with an honest store that isn't trying to skin every farmer who comes to town. Clearwater Branch has joined three other Alliance branches in starting the venture, and Charlie has been going the rounds to talk the matter up.

Honest credit, at rates that folks can afford. Free silver—or better still, greenbacks. She has learned so much these past few weeks. Speculation, railroad trusts, and middle men. A lot more happens in the world than a person would ever suspect. She gives the stew a final stir and slides the pot to the back of the range.

"Sophie?" she goes to the stairs and calls. "Would you please see that Ida and Jeffrey get themselves washed up? And then come on down yourself—it's almost dark, and I believe I hear your daddy and the boys out yonder to the barn."

"Just a minute," Sophie calls down.

The lamp is already lit, and everyone else is in place before Sophie makes her appearance. She has put on her Sunday frock and tied a ribbon around her throat, and there's a change in the way she's fixed her hair: swept into a knot atop her head, with one soft ringlet arranged in front of each ear. Sophie's hair doesn't naturally curl.

"Why, goodness gracious! Look what my little sister has gone and done!" Little Charles exclaims, the first to speak.

Sophie ignores him and slides into her seat, but immediately rises again.

"Mama, you want any help?"

"No, not tonight, but thank you just the same," she answers. "It's your birthday."

Charlie looks around to make sure that everyone is settled before he begins the grace.

"Lord, bless this food to our nourishment," he prays.

But ahead of the usual amen, he adds: "And, Lord, we beseech you to bless this daughter of ours, and to give her a soul to match the fair countenance that Thou has bestowed her with."

Charlie picks up his spoon to taste the stew.

"Would somebody kindly pass me the salt," he says.

Charlie begins to eat.

"Well?" Sophie says.

"Well what?" Charlie replies.

"Well, Daddy, do you like it or not?"

"Let me see," Charlie says, leaning for a closer look. "Yes, I believe I do like it—fact is, it's mighty becoming. And you can take my word for it because I know a pretty woman when I see one. I married your mother, now didn't I?"

"Lord help us, Charlie—listen to you now!" she says, crumbling cornbread for the baby. "I thought you married me because you were tired of eating your own fixings! That's what you said, at any rate."

"Had you fooled, now didn't I?" Charlie teases back. "Well, scripture says that modesty in a woman is a welcome thing—and naturally I didn't want to lead my own wife to perdition!"

Lately, Charlie has been in a buoyant mood, and his good will percolates down through the children too. During last week's rain, when they all had to stay inside, Charlie spent one entire afternoon in front of the fire, whittling spoons and singing an assortment of hymns. It gave her pleasure to hear him, as she stood ironing in the kitchen.

When the stewpot is empty, she slices the cake and passes the pieces around.

"Sixteen is a girl's special year," she says. "At least that's what folks claim."

"Sweet sixteen, and never been kissed!" Little Charles says. "Or *have* you, little sister?"

She looks down the table at Sophie. The girl gets heavy teasing, with so many brothers around. Occasionally it mows her down, but most times Sophie can hold her own.

"Why, *certainly* I've been kissed!" Sophie retorts, tilting her head so that the lamplight gleams on her curls. "Jeffrey and Ida kiss me every night—now don't you, sugar pies? But I expect *you* know something about kissing yourself!"

Little Charles flushes. He is a good-looking boy, and he still has his granddaddy's red hair. Little Charles seems to have more than a passing interest in one of the Wilkerson girls, but she hopes he's not working around to being serious yet. It's hard for a boy to rein in his passions, but Little Charles won't be twenty-one for another two years. He ought not to even think of tying himself down—but then it's not always up to a mother to say, and maybe that's just as well. Aaron, she suddenly remembers, was exactly the age of Little Charles when he first came courting, all those long years ago.

"Heavens, but I nearly forgot!" she exclaims aloud, jumping up from the table and rushing upstairs.

Out of breath from climbing the stairs so fast, she returns with a package that is wrapped in brown paper and string, the way it came from the dry goods store.

"It's linen," she explains, as Sophie lifts out the folded white cloth. "It's a length of Irish linen to make yourself a pair of pillow shams. When I turned sixteen, my great-aunt Dorcas gave me a piece of linen just like that, and I made up the prettiest shams you ever saw, with tatting along the hems. But when the Yankees came busting through, they carried my hope chest away, and I never laid eyes on those shams again."

She sighs, and lifts the baby Sparta from her high chair.

"I have always hoped," she says, settling the baby in her lap, "that whichever Yankee lady got those shams made good use of them."

"I doubt it," Charlie says, pushing back from the table. "More'n likely they wound up in a ditch somewhere, or else they were used to wipe down a mule."

"Anyhow, Mama, I thank you," Sophie says.

"Well, daughter, I haven't given you *my* present yet," Charlie says.

He stands up to reach into the back pocket of his trousers, pulling out a handful of coins. He counts aloud as he lines up each coin along the table edge. Sixteen silver dimes, shining in the lamplight.

"For *me*?" Sophie exclaims. "Are all of those dimes for *me*? I've never been so rich! Why, I could practically make me a necklace out of all those pretty dimes!"

"Yep, all yours," Charlie says. "You can do what you want with them, although I *would* like to offer just a word of advice. As you well know, having coins to jingle isn't something we can always count on, so I suggest you save these for the future—or invest them in something worthwhile."

"Let me guess," Little Charles interrupts. "What would be a good investment? Why, maybe her own personal share in the new Alliance Exchange!"

Charlie gives Little Charles a silencing look. About some things Charlie never teases.

"Daughter, it's up to you," Charlie repeats. "But remember, you *could* do a heap sight worse than investing in the Exchange. Hairdos and pillow shams are all right—but fact is, daughter, I can't think of any better way for you to mark your womanhood than to walk along the Alliance road."

"Good heavens, yes!" she herself chimes in, pausing on her way to put the baby to bed. "And next thing you know, *you* can be secretary of Clearwater Branch, and then I can enjoy the meetings again!"

"But, Lina," Charlie protests, "I thought you said you didn't really mind—that you were proud to be doing your part."

"Don't you worry, Charlie, my husband," she says, still holding the baby but resting her free hand lightly on Charlie's head. "I *am* proud, all right. I'm proud of our Alliance, and proud of you, and proud of all our children—and I'm especially proud of this grownup daughter who looks so pretty tonight."

Chapter 25

August 1888

Pray that it won't rain, and that it won't be too hot. Pray there'll be food enough, and that there'll be no poisonous snakes out in Will Johnson's field. She has lain awake half the night, worrying about one thing or another, but now that the first hint of dawn is showing through the windows, she suddenly wants nothing more than to roll over and sleep.

Except, of course, that she has to use the chamber pot, so she might as well get up and go outside to the privy. Why she has such a case of green apples is a mystery, since she has eaten no apples at all this week. This rumbling in her innards is probably nerves, pure and simple. Charlie thinks several hundred people will come to hear Colonel Polk speak today. He says that every farmer who's aware of anything at all will be in Will Johnson's field.

She slides from bed and leans over to find her shoes but immediately realizes that nature is calling *now*. Barefoot and in her rumpled nightgown, she hurries downstairs and out the back door, running across the wet grass and reaching the privy just in time. Well, pray it doesn't keep up like *this* all day, although Charlie's committee has dug a privy at the far end of the field. Charlie has been over there a dozen times this week, building the speaker's platform and hauling benches from the schoolhouse and pews from every church within five miles.

Clearwater Branch is sponsoring the event, but every nearby Alliance has been invited to attend—she wrote the letters herself. And then, with considerable advice from Charlie, she penned the letter to Colonel Leonidas Lafayette Polk, asking him to speak, or to find someone else who would. Colonel Polk publishes *The Progressive Farmer* and is truly the farmer's friend.

It made her mighty nervous, writing to someone famous, whose name she sees in print. She had to copy the letter over twice, before it would do. But her effort was rewarded, because Colonel Polk's reply, agreeing to speak, was addressed to her. She pasted that letter in the notebook that she uses for the minutes, and at the last meeting she passed the book around so everyone could see.

Merciful heavens! Will she need to take minutes *today*, in the midst of everything else? She has given it no thought until now, but if Colonel Polk is coming all this way to speak, then surely somebody ought to write down what he says. She'd best put her notebook and pencil into the basket with the other supplies. A thousand things to do, before they depart for Will Johnson's.

She is frying a second panful of chicken by the time Charlie and the children sit down to breakfast.

"At least it doesn't look like rain," she says, turning the chicken as it browns.

"Not today!" Charlie gloats. "I told you it would turn out fine! I told you the Lord Himself was on our side!"

"Brother Holt," she says, "I'm glad you can be so certain about which side the Lord is on, because *I* have always heard that sunshine and rain are dispensed both to those who are just and to those who are evil."

160

"Well, look who's preaching today!" Charlie teases, pushing back from the table. "We let you womenfolk in the Alliance, and next thing we know, you're liable to start taking charge of the gospel too."

He reaches out to grab the baby Sparta, who has just learned to walk and who delights in wandering under foot. He is wiping the child's breakfast from her face when a wagon pulls into the yard. Byron Weeks, one of Will Johnson's croppers, appears at the door with an envelope.

"Will's brother has just took sick!" Charlie exclaims when he's read the note. "And he and his wife have to go over there."

"Sick real bad?" she asks. "Is it his brother that lives to town?"

"He doesn't indicate—but he says for *me* to go into town and pick the Colonel up! And he hopes that *you* won't mind to give him some dinner tonight!"

"Charlie Holt, you don't mean right *here*?"

She realizes, from the startled looks on the children's faces, that she is nearly shrieking, and she makes an effort to control her voice.

"Colonel Leonidas Polk coming to this house today? When everything's torn up from all our roaring around?"

"It looks that way," Charlie replies. "And now, if you'll excuse me, I'd better start hitching up the buggy."

There's food a-plenty, despite her holding back one cake to serve the Colonel for supper, but there are flies a-plenty too, and it's hot as blazes, sitting here in the sun. Still, that hasn't diminished the crowd. Every bench is filled, and folks are sitting on quilts all around. Everywhere, people are fanning themselves, and most of the men have rolled up their shirtsleeves, except for the Colonel and Charlie, on the platform, both of whom persist in keeping their jackets on. Above the length of the platform stretches a banner, made by Sophie and two other girls, with NATIONAL FARMERS' ALLIANCE appliquéed in red.

Brother Hosea Weaver, the chaplain of Clearwater Branch, winds up a lengthy prayer—his second for the day, since he also blessed the food they ate. Then Charlie steps up to the lectern. She leans forward, nervous on his behalf, but has no trouble hearing his words.

"This crowd today," Charlie begins, "puts me in mind of *another* crowd that was sitting on a mountainside some nineteen hundred years ago—and I wonder if that day was as all-fired hot as this. But when you're listening to someone who's saying exactly what you need to hear, then it doesn't matter one iota about the heat!"

Applause breaks out all around. Spirits are high this afternoon, and it doesn't take much to bring on rousing cheers. Charlie acts like it's the most natural thing in the world to speak before a crowd like this.

"And I know that our speaker today," he continues, "is going to bring us *exactly* what we folks need to hear. Colonel Leonidas Lafayette Polk needs no introduction to any farmer in this state—so here he is!"

Another burst of applause resounds over the field as the Colonel steps forward. He is a man of medium build, with a length of whiskers sprouting from his chin. He does not look like a farmer but like a city man, and his words flow so freely that he appears to have made this speech a dozen times before. With the notebook open on her lap, she tries to keep up with the gist, but she hasn't the faintest idea of how to spell some of the words he uses. Fortunately, most Clearwater folks are getting the message first-hand.

"When I travel around this vast country," Colonel Polk is saying, "when I visit our great cities, *everywhere* I see prosperity and mammoth enterprises! I see locomotives hurtling from one end of this country to the other—I rode such a train today. I see steel rails and steam power and printing presses—and they have *revolutionized* our world!"

Silence in the crowd. Even the babies are hushed as everyone listens to this man who has traveled so far and seen so much, who speaks to both the great and the small.

"*Never* has manufacturing been so active!" he shouts. "*Never* have cities flourished so greatly! *Never* have fortunes been so easily grasped! And yet, my friends, candor compels me to say that there is something WRONG with our country!"

He leans upon the lectern, his dark eyes assessing the crowd, as though sizing up their collective strength.

"Because *never* has AGRICULTURE languished the way it does today!"

Applause thunders up, and the Colonel waits for silence before he proceeds again.

"When will this country learn that *all* our ships of commerce, and *all* our vast machinery—yes, *all* of it, I say—depends upon the muscle and strength of the AMERICAN FARMER!"

Again he waits for the clamor to cease.

"Brothers and sisters," he says, "*agriculture* is drooping and languishing and falling behind in the race! But the farmers of this great nation are growing *alert* to the threat of impending ruin! They are girding themselves to fight for relief! And I assure you that the calmest deliberation, the purest patriotism, and the most heroic courage are needed to solve the problems before us today!"

His mood shifts.

"But, brothers and sisters, I'm afraid I have sad news to bring you. Most of you here today raise *cotton* on your farms! And when autumn comes, you pick that cotton and you haul it to the gin to be baled for market—now don't you?"

The clapping affirms his assertion.

163

"And the bagging that's used to bale your cotton is made of *jute*, now isn't it? And *last* year that jute bagging cost you roughly seven cents a yard—is that correct?"

More affirmation.

"Well, brothers and sisters, I regret to inform you to-day that the jute manufacturers have gotten together among themselves—and *they* have decided that *this* year you farmers will pay *twelve* cents a yard to bag your crop!"

Anger ripples the crowd.

"TWELVE CENTS A YARD, brothers and sisters! Those big jute manufacturers think they've devised a wonderful scheme for getting rich off you-know-who. But, my friends, do *you* think it's a good idea?"

NO! NO! NO! People everywhere leap to their feet and subside again only when Colonel Polk raises his hand.

"Well, let me tell you something, brothers and sisters! I expect the farmers of this state are going to do a little whispering and conniving of their own! I expect those jute manufacturers are in for a surprise! I expect we farmers are on the verge of discovering *new* ways to bag cotton—there's nothing that says a bale of cotton has to be bagged in *jute!*"

The response is immense. All it would take is a wave from the Colonel and everyone here would march straight into town—or straight to Raleigh, if need be. As she leaps up to clap, the notebook slides from her lap. She stoops to pick it up and realizes that she has not recorded *one word* upon the page for the last considerable while. She has been so engrossed that she forgot to write. Chagrined, she sits back down and starts to scribble, while the Colonel's words still echo over the field.

He has praised her biscuits and pear preserves, and now he accepts the slice of cake she offers. The Colonel seems weary, and the dust of the afternoon has left its mark on his once-clean shirt. Much of this meal has been eaten in silence, the children too awed to speak, and Charlie is unnaturally quiet. He seems preoccupied. Will the Colonel think them ungracious?

"Mrs. Holt, you produce a mighty fine cake," the Colonel says, laying down his fork. "I would venture to say it's the best walnut cake I've ever eaten, except *that* particular honor is always reserved for Mrs. Polk."

"Thank you, sir," she replies. "But I expect you've already noticed that this cake is one of yours."

The Colonel seems puzzled.

"You printed the recipe in *The Progressive Farmer* a few months ago," she explains.

"I see," the Colonel says.

"Well, there's plenty *more* cake," she says. "Sir, I believe this slice has got your name written on it."

Obligingly, he passes his plate back down the table. The roses Sophie cut this morning are already drooping from the heat. She is embarrassed to entertain this great man in such a humble way, but it can't be helped.

"Sir, do you have any children?" she asks, trying to keep the conversation flowing in a normal way.

"Yes, I do," he replies. "All daughters. The Lord has provided me with a half dozen lovely girls, and the middle one is about the age of this fine young woman here."

He smiles at Sophie, who is pouring him another glass of iced tea. Sophie responds with a smile in return, just as Charlie, silent all this while, suddenly comes back to life.

"Pine straw?" Charlie blurts out. "Corn shucks? Honeysuckle vines? Fact is, even cotton itself would do!"

Has Charlie lost hold of his senses? But the Colonel snaps to attention, all trace of weariness gone, his eyes afire as he leans towards Charlie.

"Brother Holt," he says, "I like the sound of this. Keep talking—I can see you're a man of ideas."

"Those jute manufacturers think we're a bunch of fools!" Charlie says. "They think we're too slow and ignorant down here to catch on to their dirty tricks! Well, we dullards will just have to show them a thing or two!"

Chapter 26

October 1888

They are eating breakfast early. She has fried up a double amount of ham and baked two batches of biscuits, so there'll be food enough to pack for lunch as well. Everyone is dressed in their Sunday best, even the baby, and the excitement that flickers around this table is so bright that it outshines the lamp.

She has to eat something herself. She *must* eat. Then she'll wash the dishes and walk through the house one final time to make sure that everything is in place. It wouldn't be right, traveling to Raleigh on a pleasure excursion, if her house were in disarray. This is a momentous day. Charlie said hang the expense, that *all* the Holts are going to the State Agricultural Fair. This is Alliance Day, and the railroad is running an extra train. Half of Clearwater Branch plans to attend.

She splits open a biscuit and scoops out the soft inner part. She forces herself to swallow, feeling the biscuit's journey into her abdomen—and feeling too the grab of nature in response. What should she do? If she *doesn't* eat, she'll be too weak to troop all over the fairgrounds. But if she *does* eat, then she'll have to keep answering nature, and how does one go to the privy when traveling on a train? Do they have chamber pots on board, or do they stop once in a while, so folks can head for the woods?

She'd best not go. It's clear that she has no business to go off on pleasure, when she's feeling like this. She'd best stay home and not hinder the others' enjoyment—but she accedes only with reluctance. *Why is this happening to her? Why must her abdomen behave so mercilessly?* She has been looking forward to this trip for weeks.

"All right," Charlie is saying, "we'd better get organized, because I don't want to come home again and find any of you missing. We'll split ourselves up in pairs. Robbie and Jimmy-Jack, you two latch together, and Aaron and Jeffrey. Sophie, you hang onto Ida. I reckon your mother and me, between us, can see to the baby."

"What about Little Charles?" Aaron wants to know.

"Well, if Miss Emma Lou Wilkerson is there—and I have every good reason to expect she will be—then I expect Little Charles will shortly find himself a hand to hold."

Little Charles laughs with the rest. His courting of Miss Emma Lou has become an accepted fact.

She leaves the half-eaten biscuit on her plate and sips coffee instead.

"Mama, are you all right?" Sophie looks up to ask. "You've eaten scarcely anything."

"Your mama's too excited to eat," Charlie says. "She's not used to making a trip like this—fact is, there's *none* of us used to it. But, Lina, you don't need to worry about the train. It's as safe as any other way of getting someplace, and it sure beats walking to Raleigh!"

"Charlie," she says, almost whispering, "I don't believe I'll be going to the fair after all. I believe I'd best stay home. I seem to be having another spell."

All eyes are upon her. Ida climbs down from her chair and comes immediately to sit on her mama's lap. Charlie looks startled but does not protest, the way she assumed he would. Instead, a knowing expression crosses his face. *He thinks she's expecting again.* He thinks that's why she has to make so many trips outside, and why she can only pick at her food. Well, *is* she expecting? Does that account for the discomfort she's been having this fall? It would certainly be a relief to know what's causing these spells. Still, if she is expecting, then it's different from all the other times. She has none of the usual signs. Her breasts aren't tender, and her monthlies continue, although she's heard of women fooled in that respect. And she's been having these spells for weeks now—ever since the Colonel's picnic, in fact—and surely by now she ought to know if she's carrying a child. No, she is *not* expecting.

"You folks had better get going," she says briskly, "or else you're liable to miss that train. There's no need to sit here staring at me and let the occasion slip by. I'll be perfectly all right."

With effort, she makes a show of rising from the table and bustling the dishes away. Charlie follows her into the kitchen.

"Now you won't have to worry about hauling Sparta about," she says to him. "The child can stay home with me."

"No," Charlie says, "Sparta is coming too—between the bunch of us, we can keep up with her. Besides, you won't get any rest if you keep chasing a youngun all day—and, Miss Lina, my sweet honey, I want you to rest and take care of yourself, do you hear?"

She is relieved, frankly, but as she lifts Sparta and gives her a hug, for some peculiar reason she finds herself fighting back tears. She does not understand why. Not for herself, surely, and not entirely for having to miss the fair. Mostly for dear sweet Sparta, with her round face and dark eyes, already wiggling to be off and running again. You can't hold back a child, once they've started to grow.

"You folks be careful!" she calls out one final time as Little Charles shouts to the mules, maneuvering the wagon into the road.

The sun has not yet risen above the trees, but it promises to be a cloudless day. She stares after the wagon until she can no longer discern the separate faces of the children. *Lord, bring them back,* she prays. *Spare them from harm today.* What if she should never see Charlie and the children again? Maybe she should have gone, nature or not. But no, she admits, turning to go back inside, chilled from the unsunned air, she was wise to stay home. Already she's feeling drained. Just climbing the back steps requires a conscious exertion. How could she possibly walk the grounds of the State Agricultural Fair?

She has taken off her Sunday dress and changed back into her everyday calico, but she remains fully clothed—except for her shoes—as she lies on top of her and Charlie's bed. She does not climb under the covers—to do so would be to acknowledge that she is truly sick—but she has wrapped her arms in a shawl. She dozed a bit earlier but now is awake again. She is not sleepy, nor does her abdomen hurt at this moment, and yet she wants nothing more than to lie here and rest.

Sunlight has reached the south window, edging part of the sash but not yet penetrating the room to warm the walls and floor. It must be close to noon, and where are Charlie and the children now? Are they wandering about, looking at pigs and needlework, at all the things she so much wanted to see?

It's strange to lie here in the daylight, with the house empty and quiet. She does not recall ever, in all these years, being in this house alone. There are creaks and noises that she's never been aware of before. Something strikes the porch roof, an acorn perhaps. This day is like an island in the ordinary flow of time. She lies with her hands folded, knowing that all the beds are made, the floor swept. It is a strange luxury, this time of suspension, as though she were about to depart on a journey, her luggage already packed, but is left momentarily with nothing to do.

She ought to force herself up and find some useful task, like hemming the dress she is making for Sparta, but she hasn't the power to muster herself off this bed. Drained and useless—*but why?* Again she asks: Could there be a child? She presses her hands against her lower belly, but finds no indication of life within. Nothing. She touches her breasts, her chest, all over her abdomen, probing for some clue, some hidden cavern of pain that will show her what is wrong. She finds nothing. There is apparently nothing wrong.

And yet, there *must* be something, because she can scarcely sustain a full day's energy any more. And she keeps having these spells—not every day, thank goodness, but often enough to know that the problem is not going away. Could she have yellow fever? Malaria? The ague? But she experiences no fever or chills. Consumption? Pleurisy? She takes a deep breath and expels the air slowly, but finds no difficulty there. Is something wrong with her heart? She lays one hand on her chest and feels the thumping, feels her ribs rising and falling in a perfect normal way. Does some strange poison flow through her veins? When Charlie and the children return, will they find her lying here, with her hands neatly folded, already stiff and cold?

She must stop this nonsense. She will think of something beautiful and warm—Sparta's soft curly hair, or the cat when it purrs. She'll concentrate on that band of sunlight against the wall. She must not brood. Everything is fine. And by tomorrow—or surely by the day after that— she'll be back to her usual self again.

By evening enough strength has returned to see her through feeding the chickens. She has put some yams in the oven, and her biscuit dough is rolled and cut, ready to slide into the stove as soon as she hears the wagon. She is hungry now, and if the others don't get here soon, she'll pull out one of those yams and eat it herself. The sun has been gone for nearly an hour, and she has lit a lamp in the kitchen, where she sits in the rocker, stitching Sparta's frock.

Was that the sound of a mule? She leaps to the window. Her folks are home again! She rushes outside, receiving into her arms the child Sparta, asleep. Ida too has to be carried inside, but the others are all talking at once.

The little girls are immediately put to bed, but everyone else sits down to eat. Jeffrey, who's seven, tells her about the giant balloon they watched ascend to the sky, with two men waving from a basket below—he is still so keyed up that he's like a balloon himself, floating above the earth. This is a day the child will always remember. She would have liked to see that balloon herself.

"Old Zeb Vance made a speech," Charlie says. "We weren't up too close, but we could hear most of what he said. Everybody clapped and hollered. It was a right good speech—the kind we farmers like to hear."

"Did you see Colonel Polk?" she asks.

"No, we didn't," Charlie replies. "Course, it was a good-sized crowd, and you couldn't make out everyone there. But someone said that one of the Colonel's daughters took sick with the typhoid a few days ago."

"Well, the Lord have mercy upon the man," she softly exclaims. "I wonder if it was the daughter who's the age of Sophie here."

But Charlie does not know.

"We saw a wedding too!" Aaron reports. "They were right up on the stage, in front of everyone!"

"A wedding? At the fair? Why, I never heard of such a thing!"

"Oh, it was a sure-enough wedding, all right," Charlie explains, peeling another yam. "It was an Alliance affair,

171

and the bride was all fancied up in cotton sacks. She looked right pretty too, and we all clapped when the thing was through."

She smiles, sorry to have missed it. Why should people bag their crop in jute, when cotton sacks will do? Why, cotton sacks can even serve as a bride-dress. Charlie declares that this year's crop can rot in the fields before he bags a single pound in jute. Fortunately, he won't have to go to such extreme. A Clearwater committee has been in discussion with all the gins around. It's taken a lot of convincing to make folks realize that the farmers mean what they say, but last week one of the gins agreed to go the Alliance way.

"We've been after Little Charles all the way back home," Sophie gleefully says. "When he and Emma Lou get married, we want *them* to dress in cotton sacks! I told Emma Lou I'd help make her dress—I already have an idea for what she could do. But we want them to wait until May, so they can have the wedding in Will Johnson's field, and we can invite Colonel Polk to come again!"

Everyone laughs, and she laughs too. Little Charles is good-natured about it all. She suspects it won't be much longer before he and Emma Lou *do* get married. She suspects they're already making plans, although nothing's been formally spoken as yet. Little Charles is only twenty, but she doubts that Charlie will hold the boy to voting age.

"And how is Emma Lou?" she asks Little Charles.

"Just as pretty as always," Little Charles replies. "She said she's mighty sorry that you couldn't be with us today. She hopes you're feeling better and will soon be back to snuff. She said for me to tell you that."

There is silence around the table. All of the children, and Charlie too, look earnestly towards her.

"Yes, Miss Lina," Charlie says, "we *all* missed you today. But did you get some rest, like I told you to? And how are you feeling now?"

"Oh, I'm fine," she answers. "It wasn't much, after all—just another spell—and I'm starting to perk up again. There's no call to worry yourselves about me. But I sure do regret having to miss that fair!"

"Well, there's always next year," Charlie promises.

"Next year for sure," she says.

Chapter 27

February 1889

It's been raining for the past three days, and if it keeps up like this much longer, Charlie will have to build an ark and load in the stock, two by two. At least this was not a preaching Sunday, because she doubts that the wagon would have made it. Nonetheless, despite the weather, Little Charles set out an hour ago for a visit to the Wilkerson house. She hopes he doesn't catch pneumonia from such stubborn devotion, but now Emma Lou will get a chance to see what *better or worse* is all about, because Little Charles is bound to resemble a drowned rat by the time he arrives. Little Charles plans to marry Emma Lou in May, as soon as the planting is done.

She sighs, and hitches her chair closer to the window so that the light falls upon the newspaper in her hands. She has to hold the paper at arm's length and squint her eyes in a particular way in order to make out what it says. It's hard to distinguish the shape of the type on the page.

> MRS. WYNDHAM'S STOMACH SALTS!
> Cleanse your stomach of sour food! Purify your bowels!
> Remove foul gases! Eliminate excess bile...!

There are a dozen similar advertisements, and she studies each in turn. She has one dollar of egg money and must use it wisely. Pills, tonic, or salts—she has not yet determined which. But first she must decide which of these maladies most closely resembles her own. She needs *something*, that's for sure—something to stave the flux and perk her up again.

"Lina, it must be mighty bad news, to set you frowning so."

Guiltily, she folds the paper and looks up. Charlie is sitting by the fire, whittling a doll bed for Ida. Years ago, Charlie made a rule that no work of any sort would be done on the Sabbath, except for feeding the stock or fixing meals. However, he has also determined that while whittling an ax handle is work, making a toy is not. The same rule applies to Sophie, who's upstairs sewing. Making a dress is work, but embroidering it with flowers is not. Sometimes there's a mighty thin line between what's acceptable and what is not.

"It's the light," she answers Charlie now. "Or my poor eyes. I don't seem able to read as good as I used to."

She opens the newspaper again and makes a great show of turning the page.

"I see where Colonel Polk gave a big speech at Kinston the other day," she says. "He proclaimed that we're making a considerable dent against jute."

"Lina, I'm surprised you care," Charlie answers.

Her mistake. She should have known better than to mention the Farmer's Alliance, because Charlie still has not forgiven her for begging off from last week's meeting. It was the second time she's missed since Christmas, and she had to send the notebook with Sophie, for taking down the minutes. Even worse, in Charlie's eyes, was the fact that she offered no excuse, since she refused to admit how truly ill she felt that day. She is determined *not* to be one of those women who always whine and complain. Besides,

175

she would be too embarrassed to discuss the particulars of her ailment.

"I care, Charlie," she says quietly. "I still care, and I told you so at the time. You can still count on me to hold up the Alliance side of things."

"Well, you have a mighty strange way of showing it," he retorts.

She hates an argument worse than anything, and today, especially, she does not feel up to one. Although Charlie is almost shouting, she hears him as though he were far away, or as though her ears were stuffed with cotton. She has almost grown accustomed to this nuisance with her bowels, has learned to make allowances for that, but every few weeks some new annoyance is added to her other complaints. Her eyes, and now her ears. A mysterious bruise here and there. All her faculties seem to be blowing away, like chaff in the wind.

"Lina, sometimes you act no better than the rest of them!" He emphasizes his words with the open whittling knife. "Backsliders, all of you! You use *every* excuse you can think of, not to carry your part of the load! Well, the Lord was *certainly* right when He spoke of seeds that fall on shallow ground! But I tell you right now, Mrs. Holt— we can't turn things around unless right many of us put down roots that are deep enough to hold through drought and storm!"

Ida and Sparta have stopped their playing and drawn close. It alarms the children to hear Charlie shout, and yet perhaps it will do him good to vent his ire, once and for all. These past few weeks have brought their ups and downs. A modest victory here, but a disappointment there. The Clearwater membership stands at ninety-seven, and yet some meetings there are scarcely more than a dozen people sitting in the room. Folks like slogans and parades, but when it comes to holding things together in between, they're not so quick to step in. Lately there's been a lot of grumbling because folks' debts still aren't cleared, and the price of cotton still hasn't risen. Patience is Charlie's theme, but most folks want their rewards right now, in countable form.

"Women!" Charlie flails on. "You think certain things don't apply to you! Well, we menfolks need you *right* behind us, if we're to keep marching on!"

"Charlie, I already said I'm sorry—and I am."

She bows her head to avoid the anger in his eyes. She is starting to cry but can't help it. Everything is just too much. She *is* sorry that she stayed home Saturday last, but how much ground did the Alliance lose, on account of her being sick that day? Sometimes it feels like the Alliance is waging a war, only this time it's not the Yankees they're fighting against, because there are Yankees in the Alliance. This time they're fighting anyone who's rich and in charge of things. Bankers, lawyers, Congressmen, cotton merchants, and railroad presidents. Everyone who believes in tight money and hard credit, backed by gold. Yes, it *is* like a war, and that must be why it's so hard. And Charlie is probably right—there's no stopping midway, once you've begun. You have to keep pressing ahead until it turns out one way or the other.

There's a hand on her lap, and she looks up. Sparta has come to see why her mother is crying. Children are always alarmed when a grownup cries. She smiles, and blinks away the tears, shaking her head to show it's nothing at all. She lifts Sparta to her lap.

"Don't you worry, my pet," she says. "There's nothing the matter, not really."

Charlie looks taken aback. Will he fire another shot, with the child right here? But Charlie takes a deep breath and exhales.

"Well, Miss Lina," he says, "I know it's not your fault. It's wrong for me to heap the blame on you. It's just that it seems like a body can never march straight ahead, without always sliding back again. And this dad-blamed weather! I declare, if it wasn't the Sabbath, I'd go out there and chop me a pile of wood, whether we need it or not!"

He stands up and lays another log on the fire, then stretches his arms over his head and flaps them once or twice.

"*Cock-a-doodle-doo!*" he crows. "Come on, children!"

Then Charlie and Ida and Sparta, all of them crowing like roosters, march into the dining room and back again. It is a funny sight—Charlie making faces and the girls in giggles. They proceed up the stairs, until overhead she can hear the heavy tread of Charlie's leg, and Sophie protesting the intrusion.

"I hope the Lord doesn't mind you acting so foolish on the Sabbath," she says, smiling, when the three of them return to the sitting room.

"If He didn't want roosters to be laughed at," Charlie says, "then He ought not to have made them so silly, now had He?"

He sits down and resumes his whittling.

"And now, Miss Lina, my sweet honey—you know what I'm thinking?"

"What's that?"

"Well, I'm thinking that we ought to pop us some corn. And then maybe you wouldn't mind cooking up some of that candy you fixed at Christmastime."

"Charlie Holt, you can't make divinity with it raining like this! It'll never set!"

The disappointment shows, his and the children's.

"All right, I tell you what," she says, rising to her feet. "I'll make some fudge, because fudge is not so particular, and if it doesn't work up, then we can just eat it with a spoon."

The rain keeps pouring, and it's dismally dark outside, but at least within this room the air is clear again.

178

Chapter 28

May 1889

Little Charles' marrying day has dawned with a clear sweet beauty, and the first sunlight is now gilding the upper leaves of the apple tree she sits beneath. Everywhere, birds are awakening and slipping into song. She has come out here to the orchard, alone, in the quietness of early morning to pray the Lord's blessing on her son. It seems only yesterday that Little Charles was a mite of a boy, held in the crook of her arm, and yet now he's flying from the nest. It has all happened so fast. She will pray for Little Charles and Emma Lou, and for their future happiness.

But even as she tries to shape the words, she knows that it is really *herself* she is praying for. Her thoughts keep returning to her overwhelming obsession of the past few days: *Something is growing inside her belly.*

She is certain of it. Something that does not belong there. Something that takes her breath away, saps her strength, and steals the food she eats. Not a human child, but something—a definite heaviness, down on the lower right side.

Worms, she decided a few weeks ago. Round worms, Aunt Essie confirmed, when consulted. Hundreds of them, clumped together in a knot, making an actual bulge. Aunt

Essie gave her a vile-tasting concoction. First, she fasted from one sunup to the next, which left her so faint she scarce had the strength to proceed. Then, on the second day, she drank the potion, though it burned her mouth so bad she could hardly swallow it down. And, Lord, if she had the flux before, she certainly had it double then! For almost a week she could barely stagger about. The house was a mess, and half her chores undone, but fortunately Charlie and the boys were so busy in the fields that they didn't notice whether the floors were swept or not.

But now she is no longer certain that it *is* worms. Yesterday, working in her vegetable garden, she was seized with the notion of a squash growing inside her. An oversized squash, like the kind that will occasionally overtake all the fruit on a vine, and draw all nourishment to itself. Nine times out of ten, a squash like that tastes bitter and is not worth pulling, but is better left to rot on the vine. Has the squash inside *her* already begun to turn putrid? Are spots of mold spreading on its underside? She presses one hand against her lower abdomen—a gesture that's become habitual now—as though her fingers might be able to discern what her eyes cannot see.

She probes, and discovers another stark truth: She is getting worse, not better. *She is going to die.*

No! She protests. There's some mistake! She is too young! Didn't her daddy live to sixty-five? Hasn't her mother already reached sixty-seven? She is not prepared to die. There are the children. And Charlie. And the bright hopeful future they're all working toward.

But twist and argue as she may, the knowledge does not disappear. She is going to die. And not in the far hazy future, but much sooner than she's ever expected. Around the next bend in the road. Or the next one after that. Nothing can be taken for granted. There is only *now*.

Two heavinesses rest inside her: The familiar one, low to the right, and a second weight, new and strange, wedged between her ribs where her heart ought to be.

She will not give way to anguish but *will* keep smiling as she moves among these neighbors and kin who have gathered at the Wilkerson house. She must not spoil Little Charles' marrying day.

She looks across the yard to where Little Charles stands with his arm around Emma Lou. They both are so healthy and young. Emma Lou is a talkative girl with smooth brown hair, who does not mind keeping up with her share of the work. Little Charles has never seemed happier than now.

Well, at least she has lived long enough to see one of her children married. But what about Sophie? What about Robbie or Jimmy-Jack? What about each of the others? Will she live long enough to see Sparta go off to school? And speaking of that baby—where *is* the child now?

She finds Sparta with Charlie and some other men, out behind the barn, watching Mr. Wilkerson uncover the barbecue pit, where a shoat has been cooking.

"Sparta, you come straight here to your mama!" she says. "This is no place for a child like you."

She tries to lift the child, but Sparta is so big now, and she herself so weak, that she has to abandon the attempt. Sparta darts right back to the barbecue pit. It's the last straw! She's dying, and the child won't even obey!

"Sparta Sue, you come right back from there!"

Despair sharpens her voice. She is about to cry. Another minute, and she'll break down entirely, right in front of these menfolk. Charlie glances sideways at her and then steps forward to pick up the child, holding Sparta tight against his shoulder until the child ceases to squirm. He lays his free arm across her shoulder and leads her away from the barbecue pit, away from the others.

"You know, Miss Lina, my sweet honey," he says as they walk, "I can't help but recall that day when it was you and me standing in front of a preacher. That wasn't so long ago, it seems to me."

She quells a sob.

"Emma Lou's a right smart girl," he continues, "though she doesn't hold a candle to you."

He sets Sparta down and watches her streak away again.

"I expect it's only natural," he says, "for a woman to turn sorrowful on her child's marrying day. My own mama shed a few tears, as I recall, and I reckon your mama did too. Fact is, I know she did."

He pauses, while she takes a deep breath and tries to gain control of herself again.

"But then, Lina," he says, "it's not like he's moving that far away. Why, he'll be close enough to hand, living in the cash-renter's house, and I expect you'll be seeing him most every day. Besides, you haven't lost a son—you've gained a daughter. Try to look at it that way."

She manages a murmur that she hopes will pass for assent, as they move together towards the crowd in the Wilkersons' front yard.

Chapter 29

September 1889

She thought Charlie was out in the corn field, but instead he's heading straight for the front porch where she sits shelling peas. These days she arranges her work to allow for a sit-down task between every stand-up chore. Standing hurts. Her legs ache, and sometimes her ankles are so swollen that she can't even lace her shoes—far worse than any of the times she was expecting a child. She can no longer get an entire stack of ironing done before she has to stop and rest again. It's certainly not the way she was raised— she believes in finishing one job before moving on to the next.

Charlie comes up to the porch and stands in front of her.

"Lina, I want to know what's the matter with you," he says. "There's *something* the matter, and I don't care if you *do* insist that you're feeling just fine!"

She looks up at him, his face full of concern, but she quickly lowers her eyes again and picks up another handful of peas. What can she say? He has to know sometime, but she wants to spare him the sorrow as long as she can.

"Do you think I haven't noticed how you've been moping around? Hardly eating anything, and always running out yonder. It's not normal, Lina—and you can't convince me it is."

She flushes with shame. Was he awake last night, then? She awoke some hours before dawn in the very act of messing all over herself, too late for the chamber pot. All over her nightgown, all over the sheets, as though she were an infant again. Is there *nothing* she can depend on any more? She tried to clean herself up, in the dark. She wanted to yank the sheets from the bed, except that would have roused Charlie, so she did the next best thing—spread two clean diapers over the spot before she climbed into bed again. She did not sleep the rest of the night, and as soon as it was light and Charlie was out of the room, she snatched those sheets right off the bed. They're out in the back yard now, soaking in the washpot, while she tries to muster strength enough for beating them against the board.

"Besides," Charlie says, "I can look at you, can't I? These days it doesn't take but one look to know that something's terribly wrong."

Instinctively her hands fly to her cheeks, as though to hide her face. For weeks she has avoided mirrors, dreading their grim reflections. Her eyes peer out from deep caverns, and her skin is abnormally pale. When she puts up her hair every morning, there's a handful left in the comb. Several months ago, when she first began losing weight, she took a certain pride in avoiding corpulence, but the process, once begun, could not be halted. Now her shoulders, elbows, and knees are sharp-angled knobs.

"Charlie, I'm sorry," she whispers. "I've turned ugly and old, and I know it."

He pulls up a chair beside her and takes the pan of peas from her lap, sets it on the floor. He puts an arm around her shoulders.

"Lina, you're always beautiful to me," he says. "Besides, *pretty* doesn't matter a hoot nor a holler—you know that."

She hides her face against his sleeve.

"Lina," he says, "I wouldn't allow one of my mules to keep on suffering the way you do. I'm fetching Doc Henderson from town. I should have done it long ago."

The last time Doc Henderson came here was three years ago, when Jimmy-Jack stepped on a nail, and it went clear through his foot.

"Charlie, there's no need to be fetching a doctor," she says. "Besides, you said the other day that none of us can spend a cent until the crop is in."

"I know I said that," Charlie replies. "But I expect Doc Henderson would settle for a bushel of corn—or else he can just wait for his money."

"Charlie Holt, don't you work up a debt on account of me!"

She thinks the matter is settled, because Charlie says nothing more. She takes the pan of peas and goes back into the kitchen, but in a few minutes, as she stoops over the washpot, she sees Charlie hitching a mule to the buggy.

"Where you heading?" she calls.

"Got some business to tend to," he says as he swings up to the buggy seat.

Something about the Alliance, she tries to tell herself, watching him roll away. But she knows it's not true.

Charlie returns, alone, before noon. The younger children are already around the table, and the older boys are washing up. She is lifting roasting ears from the kettle.

"The doctor said he'd be here this afternoon," Charlie says, coming into the kitchen. "Said he'd come directly he finishes some other matters."

"Lord have mercy, Charlie Holt!"

185

She nearly drops the roasting ear. The doctor coming, and she looks a fright, wearing a frock that's patched and faded. As soon as the meal is over, she leaves Sophie with the dishes and goes upstairs. She washes herself and puts on a fresh set of underwear, a clean dress, and her best apron.

She is sitting on the porch again, another pan of peas on her lap, when the doctor's buggy appears in the road. Charlie, who has stayed at the house instead of returning to the field, goes out to greet Doc Henderson, only it's not the same person who came before. This is a young man, with a soft brown beard, and he carries a leather satchel. She is nervous, her mouth dry. She stands up, but has to sit back down again.

"Good afternoon, Mrs. Holt," the doctor says.

This must be young Doctor Henderson—old Doc Henderson's son. He sits beside her, where Charlie sat this morning, but he edges the chair around so that he looks her straight in the face. Charlie, meanwhile, has disappeared.

"Your husband tells me you're ill," the doctor says. "He's worried about you."

"I *told* him there was no call to go worrying himself about me!"

But even as the words fly from her throat, an insistent need surges forth as well: *To tell someone...to confess this secret that she has carried alone for so long.* This young man is a stranger and couldn't be thirty years old, but he seems kind, and his brown eyes are as soft as his beard. She is lying bruised by the wayside, and he's the Samaritan passing by.

It takes her a while to speak, to find the proper words, but the doctor sits attentive and does not hurry her.

"I *have* been feeling poorly," she at last admits. "I've never felt so bad in all my life. I keep thinking that next week I'll get back to my usual self again—but I never do."

The doctor nods.

"It's the flux," she says. "It's the flux that keeps draining my strength away. Seems like I can't stand to eat more than pot liquor and applesauce, and occasionally maybe some grits, but you can't get sufficient nourishment with victuals like that—it's not substantial enough to stick to your ribs."

"Are you in pain anywhere?" the doctor asks.

"Yes, some days there's right smart pain," she replies. "Well, it comes and goes—but there's a weight in my belly that never disappears."

She touches the apron above where the heaviness lies. Doctor Henderson leans forward, alert.

"I think it's time to undress now," he says. "So I can take a look."

The afternoon sun falls unshaded into the upstairs bedroom as she lies on the edge of hers and Charlie's bed, naked except for her thin chemise, the bedsheet drawn tight to her chin. She waits with dread as she hears the doctor's step on the stairs, and she turns her head away, flushed with embarrassment, as he enters the room.

"This is pleasant weather we're having," young Doctor Henderson casually remarks as he crosses the room. "September is my favorite month, though I like October nearly as well."

Through lowered eyelids she watches him place his satchel on the bureau. He has removed his jacket and rolled up the sleeves of his starched white shirt, and he whistles beneath his breath a sentimental tune—*The Last Rose of Summer*—as he takes out his doctoring tools and arranges them neatly on the dresser scarf.

"How old are you, Mrs. Holt?" he turns to ask.

"Forty-five," she answers. "My birthday's in June."

He does not appear to share her embarrassment. It's because she's old, she decides. It's because she's old and faded, because she's pitiful and sick.

She closes her eyes as he lifts the bedsheet. There's the touch of metal against her chest, and then his hands—cool, clean, and slightly damp—are pressing into her abdomen, working in a slow circle from one side to the other. She winces in sudden pain, and hears the doctor suck in his breath as he pauses over the spot that harbors her secret. Sometimes she thinks that it isn't a squash after all, but wads of unginned cotton, crammed into her abdomen.

"It's here, isn't it?" the doctor asks. "The pain is here."

She nods, her eyes still shut, feeling a sense of relief at having the secret at last discovered. Downstairs she can hear Charlie's lopsided tread, pacing the hall from front door to back, and then in the opposite direction.

"And where else?" the doctor asks. "Where else do you feel any pain?"

"Most days my legs hurt something fierce," she says. "With the right one, it starts at the top and works down to the toes, but with the left one it's the other way around—from the foot up."

Doctor Henderson moves to the end of the bed. His hands move deftly over her ankles, pressing with his fingers everywhere. He might be a woman kneading dough or combing a daughter's hair, his touch is so certain and smooth. It gives her an odd sort of pleasure, and for a moment—just a moment—a bubble of hope swells up within her. She will get well. She will get cured, just from the healing touch of young Doctor Henderson's hands.

But he seems to have found what he was looking for, pressing against her left shin, just above the ankle. Then he abruptly hands her the bedsheet, and she draws it once more to her chin.

"I'm dying, aren't I?" she asks, though her voice comes out a hoarse whisper.

Young Doctor Henderson stands beside the bed, rolling down his sleeves. She hopes fiercely to hear a denial—

and yet, more than anything, she wants to know the truth. She has had enough hiding.

"Where there's life, there is always hope," young Doctor Henderson says. "I have read of tumors dissolving away. But I have never had such a case myself, nor my father either. And, Mrs. Holt, unfortunately it will take right much of a miracle to help you now. I'm sorry. I deeply wish it weren't so."

She nods, not trusting speech, lest it be a croak. Tears fill her eyes but do not actually roll down her cheeks. She turns her head away and lies there, silent, as she waits for young Doctor Henderson to pack up his tools again, and even after he leaves the room, quietly shutting the door behind him, she lies unmoving on the bed. She feels no pain at this moment—only weariness, and a sharp furious sorrow, to which she must not give in. She hears nothing, not the sound of voices, nor children playing, nor the doctor's buggy departing. She has no sense of how much time has passed before she rises from the bed and slips this morning's calico over her head.

Downstairs, as she steps onto the front porch, Sophie leaps to her feet and lays her sewing aside.

"Mama, you sit right here, and I'll bring you some tea," the girl says. "I offered some to the doctor, but he declined."

She shakes her head in refusal. Will they all start treating her different now?

"Where is your daddy?" she asks.

"He and the doctor walked over yonder," Sophie says, pointing towards the orchard. "The doctor came back a while ago and got in his buggy and left, but Daddy's still out there, I reckon."

Charlie is not in the orchard. Moving slow, to favor the pain, she threads her way across the potato field and into the woods beyond. Through the dying leaves she spies a blue shirt. Charlie sits hunched on a log, his back to her, but he turns around at the sound of her approach. His face is swollen and blotched. He has been crying.

She sits on the log beside him and takes his hand.

"I didn't realize!" he blurts out. "This is the cruelest blow I ever had. I *love* you, Lina! I *need* you! The children need you! It's just not fair!"

"Hush, Charlie," she says, stroking his hand. "Hush, now. It's not a case of what's *fair*, Charlie—or cruel either. It's a case of what *is*—and of what's going to be."

Chapter 30

Christmas Day, 1889

She has planned the menu for weeks and has copied out each recipe she will need, not trusting her memory any more. Baked ham and roast capon—she will use both ovens. Collard greens, turnips, and a mixture of rice and peas. Mashed potatoes with red-eye gravy. Sweet potatoes and sausage, baked together in a recipe clipped from *The Progressive Farmer*. Spoonbread and biscuits. And then finally her Japanese fruitcake and two kinds of pie.

None of it will she be able to eat.

Alone in the kitchen, before anyone else is awake, she dresses by lamplight. Shivering in the chill, she eases a stocking over the lump on her lower left shin, a lump that's nearly the size of an egg. Her body's garden is growing wild, and weeds spring up wherever they choose. But the more chaotic that garden becomes, the more she herself craves order and routine, and the more she takes pleasure in ordinary deeds, performed in a normal way. Laying the table for a meal. Sewing on a button. Churning butter and patting it into the carved wooden mold.

And yet, each week that goes by, she is less and less able to perform even such simple tasks to her own satisfaction. Increasingly she has to rely on the strength of others—on Charlie and Sophie and the boys—just to get her housework done. The pain in her legs has become so intense that she can no longer even bear standing in the yard and stretching clothes along a line. But having to ask for help hurts her more than anything. Still, she is trying to accept what has become her lot. Above all, she must never complain. Especially on Christmas Day.

Rising painfully, she struggles to lift the ham that has been soaking overnight in a pail of water. If she doesn't start working on dinner now, the meal won't be ready by the time everyone arrives.

"Lina, what in the name of all tarnation are you doing up so dad-blamed *early?*"

Charlie, in his winter underwear, stands in the doorway.

"Getting things started," she replies, opening the oven and then trying to hoist the pan in which she's placed the ham.

She gives up the endeavor for a moment to catch her breath before trying again, but Charlie steps forward and seizes the pan from her hands. Easily he slides it into the oven.

"Here," he says. "You ought to know better than to try and lift such a thing. Sometimes, Lina Holt, you are the beatenest woman I ever saw. And what are you out here cooking for? Don't you know it's Christmas? You ought to be still in bed, resting up for today."

"Why, of course I know it's Christmas! What do you think I'm out here for? I don't intend for folks to eat leftover cornbread for Christmas dinner!"

She sits down and checks her list to see what to do next: mix up the dressing to stuff the birds.

"Lina, I *told* you not to worry about fixing a dinner. When I wrote folks to come, I asked them each to bring a basket of food, on account of the circumstances."

"Charlie Holt, you didn't! Lord, but I am ashamed!"

Charlie lays his hands on her shoulders.

"Miss Lina, my sweet honey—don't you know it's *you* they're coming to see? I don't want you all tuckered out before they even arrive."

The sage and the parsley are across the room. Everything she needs is always across the room. She sighs, and gets to her feet, but Charlie nudges her down again.

"Tell me what you want, and I'll fetch it. And then I'll go wake Sophie up, to come help."

"No, leave her be," she says, shaking her head. "She does so much as it is. Besides, I doubt it'll be much longer before the little ones rouse up to sniff the fact that it's Christmas Day."

She takes an onion and begins to peel it. Her eyes sting, but there is satisfaction in knowing what accounts for the pain.

"Charlie," she says, wiping her eyes on her sleeve, "I'm not trying to be ornery and perverse. It's just that once more—just this one last time—I want the pleasure of fixing a truly decent meal, and then watching folks enjoy it."

This time when she gets to her feet Charlie merely stands aside. She dollops butter into a skillet and begins frying the onions. Then she glances at Charlie and sees the stricken look on his face. Lord have mercy! She did not mean to remind him of *that*—not on Christmas Day! As the onions begin to sizzle, filling the kitchen with their pungent aroma, she touches Charlie's cheek, and he wraps her in his arms. She rests her head against the warm nap of his winter underwear.

"I tell you what, Charlie, my husband. Once I've got things under way, I'll turn it over to Sophie, and to Emma Lou, if she's here by then—and then I'll lie down and rest."

"Is that a promise?"

"Yes, it's a promise."

She awakens to voices in the hall below, to the excited pitch of children's laughter. Her brother Ben and his wife, Ellen, and their children, from the sound of it. She ought to go down and greet them, yet she cannot bring herself to roll from the bed just yet. She is far more tired than she wants to admit. These spells of fatigue come and go when they please, beyond her ability to control them. She'll lie here another minute or two.

She shuts her eyes again but opens them when the door creaks open. Is it Charlie, come to fetch her? Instead her mother tiptoes into the room.

"Daughter, you asleep?" Mama asks.

"No, come on in. I'm just being lazy and playing possum."

Mama comes over to the bed.

"Oh, my goodness, child!" Mama exclaims. "They said you were mighty thin, but I never expected *this!*"

"I look terrible, don't I?"

She swings her legs over the edge of the bed, smoothing down her petticoat so the lump on her shin doesn't show. Mama leans down, and they embrace. When they turn each other loose, Mama sits down in the rocker, filling the chair so completely that the folds of her dress puff out between the slats.

"By rights it ought to be me," Mama says. "I haven't got any little ones depending on me. And anyway, at *my* age you figure you've already had more than your share of doing."

"Mama, you'll make me feel bad if you start that. It doesn't really matter who's had the biggest share. Besides, I expect it's never convenient, even if you live to be a hundred."

"No, I guess not," Mama sighs.

Downstairs, more folks are arriving. She slides from the bed to find her shoes, but when she slips one onto her foot, without even hooking a button, she knows that she cannot tolerate the pain. Her shoes are too small and her dress too big. It's crazy to wear her Sunday best with her old house slippers of quilted calico, but it will have to do. She pulls the dress over her head and turns to Mama for assistance in fastening the back.

"Lina," Mama says, giving the skirt a final tug the way she must have done a thousand times, dressing one child or another, "you know, I'm not so old yet but what I'd be glad to stay and help, if you feel like you need me to. I'm not chipper, but I can still wash dishes and tend to younguns."

"Mama, it's not right for me to call on *you* for help, when it ought to be the other way around."

"Nonsense. You just holler, do you hear?"

How many people are in the house right this minute? Thirty-one. No, thirty-two, counting Ben's newest baby, asleep across the way. It was Charlie's task to figure where everyone would sit, and he's done an admirable job. He built an extra table out of planks and set it end-to-end with the regular one. Ben and Little Charles, who sit where the tables join, have to be careful where they set their plates.

"Ben," she calls down to her brother, "can I pass you another biscuit? There's plenty more where these came from."

"Much obliged," Ben answers.

She passes the biscuits down. Every dish she owns has been pressed into service today. There's plenty of food, and everyone is eating. But there's something missing: the natural flow of talk. The children seated in the kitchen are chattering away, but around this table, where sixteen grownups are jammed elbow to elbow, little is being said, beyond a few careful remarks about the weather and the food. Charlie has made several attempts to get things rolling, but nothing seems to catch. It's not enough, apparently, to fix the

195

table fancy and serve up a bounty of food. It's not enough for a family to gather, even on Christmas Day.

"Charlie," she says brightly, "why don't you slice some more ham and pass it around?"

"Surely," Charlie replies, and sets to work.

Suddenly it dawns on her what is wrong. It's because *she* is sitting in their midst. Who can enjoy a meal, eating in the presence of death?

What ought she do, then? Excuse herself and go lie down? She is tired enough, that's for certain. If she were to leave, would it take away this pall? Or would they start talking *about* her, and would that make things worse? Maybe it was selfish of her to want such a gathering today. Maybe she is spoiling everyone's Christmas.

Is there something she can say, to make folks less somber? She can't mention the crops just sold, since most folks were disappointed once again. And religion isn't safe, because John Sanders has recently converted to the Holiness persuasion, and Flora too. Charlie has already trodden dangerously close to that.

The National Farmers' Alliance! Why didn't she think of that before? Every single person around this table is a member of the Alliance.

"Wasn't that wonderful news about Colonel Polk?" she says.

Colonel Leonidas Lafayette Polk—*their* Colonel Polk—has just been elected president of the national organization, and he's moving to Washington, D.C., to take hold of things. Her words fall like a flower in everyone's midst, and the conversation starts to unfold. Folks shift in their places and begin to smile.

"That was splendid news, all right," her brother Ben pronounces. "That's the best news we've had for a while—and I fully expect that North Carolina's loss will prove to be the nation's gain."

196

"With the Colonel at the reins," John Sanders says, "I reckon we farmers will show the world a thing or two. We showed them jute folks quick enough, now didn't we?"

There's a chuckle of assent. This fall, the price of jute mysteriously dropped again. Some big explanation was offered, but everyone knows the reason why.

"I'll never forget the time," Charlie says, leaning back in his chair, "that Colonel Polk himself was sitting right here at this table—just like we are now—and eating one of Lina's biscuits. Said he liked it too, as I recall. That was the very first day we ever heard mention of the whole jute business. We talked about it with the Colonel, sitting right here."

"Right here?" Flora exclaims.

"Yep, right here," Charlie answers. "Fact is, Flora, the Colonel was sitting where you are now. And I said to myself that evening, after he was gone, that Colonel Polk is a mighty fine man—he's one of the *finest* men I've ever had the privilege to know. And I don't mind saying today that I am *proud* of Colonel Polk, and I'm *proud* of the Farmers' Alliance, and I'm *proud* of North Carolina too!"

"Amen!" John Sanders resounds.

She is satisfied. *This* is the Christmas meal she'd envisioned. Now there will be a New Year. Now there is hope again. Now there is something more promising to consider than the fate of one dying woman.

Chapter 31

February 1890

A shawl around her shoulders, she sits as close to the fire as she dares, but it feels like she'll never get warm. The gall on her leg is hurting something fierce this afternoon, and she is tempted to ask Sophie to fix her a dose of the laudanum that young Doctor Henderson brought. He does not want her to suffer, he says, any more than can be helped. Only twice has she succumbed to a dose during daylight, but at night she lets herself take a few drops. The medicine eases the pain, but it also makes her thoughts blur together. Her mind, her thoughts, her memories are all she has left, and now even those are slipping away. No, she will bear the pain this afternoon.

Isn't it peculiar that it's her *left* leg that has the gall and pains her so? She has heard said that if a man and woman live together long enough, they will start to resemble each other. Sometimes she wonders if this lump on her leg is her body's way of resembling Charlie. The last time Doctor Henderson was here, she asked him to saw off that leg completely, but he acted as though she was speaking in jest and said he'd no intention of doing such a thing. But she wasn't jesting. If the leg is removed, won't the pain disappear? Then Charlie could make her a *new* leg out of red cedar, to match his own. Besides, how could *no* leg be any worse than this? She can scarcely walk anyway, and has to be rolled around in the straight-backed chair that Charlie fixed up with wheels.

"Ida," she calls to the child, who's playing house with Sparta. "Could you help Mama for a moment?"

Sometimes Ida is the spitting image of her grandmother, but on a smaller scale. She has been trying to teach Ida to sew. At least she can do *that* much to prepare her daughter for the life ahead. But today her leg aches so bad that she hasn't the patience to work with the child. Maybe she will quilt for a while, to take her mind off the pain.

"Honey," she says to Ida, "would you mind to thread me a needle? Can you do that for me?"

"Of course I can, Mama!" Ida proclaims.

"Well, then bring me the thread and my scissors— they're in that basket over yonder. I'll cut off a piece, and you can poke it through."

Can't even thread her own needles now. Charlie lent her his reading glass, but it takes both hands to thread a needle. While Ida sits down on the floor and sets to work, the baby Sparta, who's not a true baby any more, comes to stand by the rocking chair.

"Mama," Sparta pronounces. "Mama."

Sometimes the child seems not entirely sure that this pale woman is indeed her mama. It's Sophie who does the real work of mothering these days, the dressing and feeding and such, but it gives her pleasure to have Ida and Sparta close by, to watch them play, to touch their soft cheeks and shining hair. Each is a beautiful flower, and it's a miracle to watch them bloom, despite the chill all around.

Sparta attempts to climb into the rocking chair. She tries to assist the child, but Sparta's wiggling makes the pain in her abdomen so intense that she can scarcely keep from crying out. The dear sweet child, and yet she cannot bear it.

"You're my Sparta," she says. "And I love you—I hope you can always remember that."

She kisses Sparta and eases her back to the floor again.

"Something's the matter with this old thread!" Ida says. "It won't go in!"

The thread is hopelessly frayed. She'll have to call for Sophie after all, though she hates to bother her for trifles. Sophie has borne many burdens these past few weeks, and it's not over yet. Occasionally Sophie's spirits fail and she shrills at one of the boys, but most days she runs this household as though it were the most natural thing in the world. There's little that she herself can do to help. She feels real bad that Sophie's girlhood must end so soon.

She will not live to see her oldest daughter wed. Any prospects have been set aside, for the duration, although she has noticed an extra flutter and blush whenever young Doctor Henderson stops by. It will pass. Young Doctor Henderson is already engaged to be married and has sense enough not to tarry where he doesn't belong.

Well, if she's denied the satisfaction of seeing Sophie wed, at least she can help the girl get ready for that eventual day. She is quilting some of the beautiful tops that Sophie has pieced. She tries to work at it several hours a day, and sometimes Sophie will join her for a few minutes, and occasionally Carrie Barnes or some other friend will stop by to see her and help for a while. Thus far, she has finished one quilt and started a second, though she has to work mainly by feel. She hopes that her stitches are straight enough that Sophie won't be ashamed some day of the work her mama has done.

"Sophie!" she calls, when she hears the girl come into the house from out in the yard somewhere.

There's a clatter in the kitchen, and then Sophie appears at the door, her cheeks bright from the wind.

"I was checking to see if the clothes are dry—but not yet. What do you need, Mama?"

"If you'll pull that quilt frame over here and thread me a set of needles, I'll work on your quilt some more."

"Mama, the world's not going to collapse if that quilt doesn't get finished right away. Don't wear yourself out. There's plenty of time."

"Daughter, it's been my experience that time isn't something you can always count on."

Sophie has threaded a half dozen needles when there's the sound of a buggy outside. Immediately Sophie looks up, and her face brightens. She smoothes down her hair and hurries into the hall.

But instead of young Doctor Henderson, it's Preacher Daniels from Mount Moriah that Sophie leads into the room. He is a thin and earnest man, with a barren wife, and he serves three churches, twenty-odd miles apart. Today, his Bible under his arm, he seems especially determined.

"I was by this way and wanted to pay you a call," he says. "Sister Holt, how are you feeling today?"

"Oh, I can't complain."

She takes a final stitch and leaves her needle inserted in the cloth, where she can find it again, then motions for Sophie to move the quilting frame away. The pain in her abdomen suddenly cries for attention, and she wishes now that she'd taken some laudanum after all, but it's too late. Preacher Daniels sits in the straight-backed chair on the other side of the hearth. He leans forward.

"Sister Holt, I've come to pray with you."

Sophie stoops to pick up a scrap of thread and then leads the little girls from the room, tiptoeing as she departs. She closes the door behind her, and Preacher Daniels opens his Bible.

"Sister Holt," he says, "I hope you're finding comfort in the scriptures during this time of trial."

"Well, some evenings my husband reads aloud to me, and yes, I do take comfort in it."

Charlie Holt, reading a Psalm, is enough to make you sing or weep, depending on the particular verse he lights upon. *The Lord is my shepherd, I shall not want....* But it's not the Psalms that Preacher Daniels turns to. He hitches his chair still closer, so that their knees almost touch, and he gives her a searching look.

"Sister Holt, there's a promise that I want to share with you today," he says, his finger marking the place. "A promise that you can hold in your heart as you walk through the valley that lies ahead. No matter how dark the day, no matter how hard the travail, you can hold this promise close."

Fervently he begins to read about a new heaven and a new earth...about a new Jerusalem, a beautiful crystal city with streets of gold...a city where sun and moon don't shine, but where the saved shall gather to bask in the light of the Lord.

At last he closes his Bible and looks up.

"Sister Holt," he says, "what do you think of that?"

"That's a beautiful place, I reckon," she replies. "I've never heard of any place to compare with it."

"Well, it's *yours*," he whispers. "It's promised to *you*, Sister Holt, because you've opened your heart to the Lord."

Then he prays at length and rises to depart. He does not touch her hand but silently steals from the room, and there's a sudden cold draft from the hall as he opens the front door. She sits alone in the dimming twilight, shivering despite the shawl. The fire on the hearth has died down and gives off little heat, but she does not call for Sophie to add more wood or to light a lamp.

Instead, she tries to contemplate this city that's soon to be hers. She has never lived in a city, has never lived anywhere except on a farm. She has never even been to Raleigh, forty-odd miles away. And it's not likely now that she'll ever see a real city on this earth—fact is, it's not likely that she'll ever leave this house again. The Holy City, the new Jerusalem, seems most unlike that cluster of houses and stores in town where she and Charlie go to trade. Why, the main street of town isn't even *paved*, much less with gold.

And why, she wonders, did the Lord Almighty choose to pave His city with *gold*, when it's gold that causes so much trouble for farmers and working folk? Ask any Alliance member—ask Charlie, for instance—and you'll hear an immediate argument for using greenbacks instead of gold.

But it's not for a poor sick woman to question what the Lord has in mind. Still, if it was up to her, she would prefer a beautiful garden where fruits and flowers grow. It would be like Charlie's orchard, only much larger, with all sorts of flowers growing in orderly fashion beneath the trees. And there would *always* be pears and apricots ripe for picking, even in the wintertime. And birds would sing, and bees would buzz in and out of their hives, and there would be no need to chop or hoe because there would be no weeds, except maybe around the edges—Queen Anne's lace and wild pink roses, a few pretty weeds like that.

And she could sit there all day, without pain, on a bench in the sun, and keep warm. Now *that* would be Paradise.

Chapter 32

April 1890

Pots and pans...cups and spoons...the floor to sweep...sweep and sweep...sweep and sweep...but there's someone else in this kitchen.....

She opens her eyes. Charlie sits beside the bed, clasping her hand. Is this winter or summer? Is it night or day? She has lost all sense of time and seems to be floating in a dark open space, moving in no particular direction.

"Charlie?" she says with effort. "What day is it? And what time?"

Still holding her hand, Charlie reaches into his pocket and pulls out his watch.

"It's morning, Lina—about quarter to eleven. And this is Wednesday. I believe it's the eighth—no, the ninth of April, and it's a right fine day. The sun's out, and it's warming up, so long as you're not in the wind."

There is something about April, something she has to do, but she cannot remember what. The planting? Does it have to do with that?

"How come you're not in the fields?" she asks, the words thick on her tongue. "You got the planting done already?"

"No, not yet," he answers. "But don't you worry yourself about *that*. I got the boys out working on it, and it will get done soon enough. Scripture says there's a time to sow and a time to reap, and we've done our share of both, Miss Lina, it seems to me. Now I reckon it's time to sit and wait."

He leans over the bed and kisses her cheek. She looks up at his face, but there's a blur where his eyes ought to be. She wants to reach up and touch his beard, to feel its sharp bristles again, but her arm is too heavy to lift from the bed. Dear Charlie. Now she remembers.

"Your birthday," she says. "It's your birthday—and, Lord, but I haven't even started your cake!"

She struggles to rise from the pillow, but Charlie gently pushes her down again. He strokes her hair. The blur has shifted a bit, and now she can see a glisten beneath his eyes.

"Miss Lina, my sweet honey, don't you fret yourself," he says. "Be good and lie still. I reckon you've baked enough cakes by now and don't have to strain yourself to do up any more."

"Coconut or lemon chiffon? Which do you want?" she whispers, even as she closes her eyes again.

"Oh, lemon chiffon, I reckon," Charlie answers from far away.

Flecks of peel...sifted flour...eight whites...stir and stir...stir and stir....

Sophie, standing beside the bed, holds a cup and spoon, and there's a clinking sound as she stirs.

"Mama, I've fixed you some hot water and honey. Do you think you can keep it down?"

Sophie and Charlie both are there. Charlie lifts her head from the pillow and holds her steady as Sophie feeds her with the spoon, one sip at a time. The familiar sweetness melts its way down, but she shakes her head. She does not want any more.

Shadows move back and forth. There's a group of people gathered in this room, and she is surprised to see her daddy among them—but the haze clears for a moment and she recognizes Little Charles, who has the same red hair. All of her children are here, and she tries to sort them out in her mind: Little Charles, Sophie, Robbie, Jimmy-Jack, Aaron, Jeffrey, Ida, and Sparta.

Charlie holds Sparta in his arms, and he lays the child on the bed. Sparta immediately crawls forward to rest on the pillow. She turns to look at the child, and they stare at each other, eye to eye. Bright dark eyes that do not blink. She tries to speak Sparta's name—but cannot. And then Charlie takes Sparta away again.

"Mama, look a-here," Sophie says, leaning over the bed and holding something before her face. "Ida has picked you a flower. Can you see?"

There's only a yellow blur where the flower should be, but the smell of a daffodil is unmistakably clear.

Spring in the orchard...trees bloom...birds sing...whip-poor-will...whip-poor-will....

Even without opening her eyes, she can sense that Charlie is alone with her now.

"What time?" she asks.

He stands up and she hears—but does not see—Charlie open his watch to consult it.

"It's midafternoon," he says. "It's half past three."

"You hear them singing?" she asks. "Do you hear all those birds?"

Charlie moves closer, and he lays a hand on her forehead.

"Birds? Miss Lina, are you sure it's not the angels you hear?"

No, it's birds. She's sure of it. Sweet and clear. Many birds, singing from high in the trees.

"Aaron was always studying the birds," she says.

"*Aaron!*" Charlie exclaims with anguish. "Lina, my sweet Lina—is it Aaron you're seeing now? Has *he* come to claim you again, even after all these years?"

He leans over the bed and cradles her in his arms. It's cold and dark in the orchard, cold and dark in the woods. No, Aaron is not here. She can scarcely remember him any more. Slowly she shakes her head. She is almost too weak to reply.

"No, Charlie," she whispers. "There's no one here but you."

Acknowledgments

Growing up, I occasionally read the *Progressive Farmer* magazine, but I had never heard of the National Farmers' Alliance until I stumbled upon an essay by Julie Roy Jeffrey on women in the Southern Farmers' Alliance (*Feminist Studies*, Fall 1975). However, once I discovered the Alliance, I immediately knew that Charlie Holt would gravitate to such an organization.

On visits home to Chapel Hill, North Carolina, I perused letters and reports of Alliance meetings in the Papers of Leonidas Lafayette Polk in the Southern Historical Collection of the University of North Carolina Library. In the same library, the North Carolina Collection yielded 1880s copies of the *Progressive Farmer*, complete with Alliance news, agricultural advice, and household hints.

The library of the University of California, Berkeley, provided innumerable other resources, including a biography of Leonidas Lafayette Polk, books on Southern agrarian movements, and various accounts of the Civil War. One perspective on the Civil War was especially vivid and useful: Katherine M. Jones, *When Sherman Came: Southern Women and the "Great March"* (New York: The Bobbs-Merrill Company Inc., 1964).

The seed money for The Days & Years Press came from the estate of my father, Robert Lee Hardison (1913–1993). My father grew up on a farm in Chowan County, North

Carolina. Although he worked for the University of North Carolina in various roles in purchasing for 57 years, I often thought of him as an "urban farmer" because gardening was always such an essential part of his life.

The Days & Years Press is based in California, but my sister, Betty Hardison, serves diligently as our North Carolina partner; in recent months she has developed first-hand knowledge of many bookstores throughout the state. My son, Lief Kaiper, continues to provide help and encouragement. One delight of this publishing venture has been working with the cover design team of Diane Goldsmith and Alison Jewett-Furlo of Square Moon and with the illustrator Barbara Epstein-Eagle, whose watercolor paintings have expanded my own perception of the women in this series.

The Story of Lina Holt was originally completed in 1981 and has received only minor textual editing since then.

G.V.K.

Gina V. Kaiper grew up in Chapel Hill, North Carolina, and graduated from the University of North Carolina. In the late 1960s, she moved to the San Francisco Bay area. She now lives in Pleasanton, California, and earns her living writing about science and technology.

OTHER NOVELS BY GINA V. KAIPER IN
THE DAYS&YEARS SERIES:

I Shall Never Speak, 1995
(ISBN 0-9645206-2-1)